William Wallace Harris

The Battle of Groton Heights

a collection of narratives, official reports, records, &c - Vol. 1

William Wallace Harris

The Battle of Groton Heights
a collection of narratives, official reports, records, &c - Vol. 1

ISBN/EAN: 9783337390280

Printed in Europe, USA, Canada, Australia, Japan

Cover: Foto ©Andreas Hilbeck / pixelio.de

More available books at **www.hansebooks.com**

THE

BATTLE OF GROTON HEIGHTS:

A

COLLECTION OF NARRATIVES, OFFICIAL REPORTS,
RECORDS, &c.,

OF THE

STORMING OF FORT GRISWOLD,

AND THE

BURNING OF NEW LONDON

BY BRITISH TROOPS, UNDER THE COMMAND OF BRIG.-GEN. BENEDICT ARNOLD,

ON THE

SIXTH OF SEPTEMBER, 1781.

WITH AN INTRODUCTION AND NOTES.

By WILLIAM W. HARRIS.

———— ✦✦✦ ————

"Zebulon and Naphtali were a people that jeoparded their lives unto the death in the high places of the field."—*Judges*, 5 *Chapt.* 18 *Verse.*

[Inscription on Monument.]

———— ✦✦✦ ————

NEW LONDON:
1870.

INDEX.

PREFATORY NOTE.

THE actors in the bloody scene at Groton and New London, on the 6th of September, 1781, have long since been gathered to their fathers, and those who with boyish awe heard its vivid recollections from their lips are becoming aged and fast following them. A fear that as with each year the event receded into the past the details would become more dim, until all that remained of its features would be the outlines in the nation's history, led to the attempt of, as far as possible, gathering all information upon the subject with a view to its preservation.

It is true that valuable and interesting accounts of this event have been given to the public, but, with the exception of Rathbone's edition of Hempstead's and Avery's Narratives, [published in 1840 and now virtually out of print,] they are embodied in large and expensive volumes of extraneous history, which by many would be thought too costly. A farther reason for publishing was, that all histories before published are but partial; extracts from reports and narratives are given—but a full and complete collection of all papers bearing upon the subject has never been made.

The writer felt that its importance in history, particularly in that of his own town and state, warranted a full account in a volume especially devoted to the purpose; a conviction strengthened by expressions of approval from friends in whose opinions he has great confidence. The plan of publication has been to present the reader with the cotemporaneous accounts as given by each side in order to allow him to draw his own conclusions regarding the event. To fully carry out this plan it is necessary to publish what it is feared will, to some, appear dry, uninteresting details, yet which to a complete work are indispensable; for example, the reports of the Court-Martial and the Memorial from citizens of New London to the Governor and Council of Safety, which, although they add no new facts of interest to the action proper, throw much light upon the actual condition of New London for defence at that time, and relieve the reputation of an officer from an unjust imputation which has, from public ignorance in the matter, clouded it to the present day.

The narrative of the late Jonathan Brooks, and especially that of the quaint John Hempsted, showing the serio-comic side of the tragedy, will, in their amusing truthfulness, it is thought, more than compensate for the barrenness and dry detail inseparable from official reports.

These narratives, as also that of Dr. Downer, have never before been published. In all of them the peculiar orthography of the authors has been scrupulously preserved, as an attempt of change to our modern style might, in some cases, also alter the sense from that intended. In the preparation of the notes in the text great care has been taken to make no statement as *positive* in which there is the least shade of doubt; when made by extract the authority is given; and when suggested by probabilities it is so expressed. H.

New London, July, 1870.

INTRODUCTION.

In the latter part of the summer of 1781 Sir Henry Clinton, commander-in-chief of the British forces in North America, became apprised, by intercepted letters,[1] written by Washington, of a meditated attack upon New York by the allied French and American forces. Acting on this information he called to his aid a considerable portion of the "Army of the South," under Cornwallis.

On this fact becoming known to Washington he immediately reversed his entire plan of proposed operation, and determined to fall upon Cornwallis with an overwhelming force before Sir Henry Clinton should be able to amend his mistake by reinforcing the Earl. Washington gladly adopted a movement in which the prospects were good of retrieving the fortunes of the American arms in the south, which, under command of General Greene, had, except in two or three unimportant skirmishes, been disastrous during the campaign of that year.

To more completely distract the attention of Sir Henry from his true design, Washington, while vigorously perfecting his plans of organization, preserved a formidable appearance of design against New York. Count de Grasse, who had recently arrived from France with a powerful naval force, was ordered to the Chesapeake to act in conjunction with an allied army which had quietly been withdrawn from the north and dispatched to that point. So discreetly and with so much secrecy was this important movement conducted that Sir Henry was not aware of it until too late to prevent, by reinforcements, its probable disastrous consequences upon his lieutenant.

On acquaintance with the fact, and realizing the impossibility of strengthening Cornwallis in time, he resolved, as a last resort, to send an expedition against a northern port still in possession of the Americans.

---

[1] Lossing supposes them to have been written for the express purpose of deceiving Sir Henry, but this supposition hardly appears to be sustained by circumstances and subsequently developed facts.

By this measure he hoped to induce Washington to recall either the whole or a great part of his expedition in order to protect the threatened point. A strong American army of observation still menaced New York, and he therefore could not prudently withdraw from its defence a sufficient force to make the attempt on a distant or strongly fortified point; yet at the same time it was necessary that the point attacked and the apparent consequence of its fall should be of sufficient importance as to divert Washington from his descent on Cornwallis.

New London, above all others, appeared the proper point. Its deep and capacious harbor, in the event of a permanent lodgment, would be unequaled as a station and rendezvous for the immense naval force expected from England in the following spring. It was within a few hours sail of New York, and in case the attack upon it should be unsuccessful the retreat would be open and safe. From its port swarmed the dreaded privateers which, while by their captures they furnished the rebels with stores and munitions with which to continue the war, at the same time cut off the supplies and weakened the royal armies' powers of offence. By the capture of the harbor their great rendezvous would be broken up. Beside these very strong reasons were others no less important. Should its reduction be followed by permanent occupation it would open a most favorable route for the invasion of central New England, for a large portion of which it was the natural port. In addition to all other incentives for its attack was the rich prospect of immediate plunder. At this time the accumulation of captured military and other stores here was immense, the cargo of the merchant-ship Hannah alone being valued at four hundred thousand dollars. The fortifications were comparatively small and inefficiently garrisoned. The regular garrisons consisted nominally of one company of artillery and one of infantry in each—Fort Trumbull on the west or New London side, and Fort Griswold on the opposite or Groton side, of the river. A small battery on Town Hill, known as Fort Nonsense, was manned by detachments from Trumbull. Captain Adam Shapley commanded the artillery, and was senior officer of the latter fort. William Latham was captain of artillery, and Oliver Coit of the infantry at Fort Griswold. Colonel William Ledyard commanded the military district, comprising the towns of New London and Groton, the harbor and its defences.

At this time the garrisons, which were very seldom if ever full, were especially depleted; most of the men who were capable of bearing arms were either in the armies operating in the field, or, as was more generally the case, were, by the force of habit and the associations of a people peculiarly maritime, drawn into either the public or private naval service.

All these advantages for attack being offered by New London, Sir Henry Clinton decided to equip a force with all possible dispatch for its reduction. Arnold had just returned from a predatory incursion on the southern coasts, and his success on that, no less than his peculiar fitness for this expedition to the neighborhood of his early home, induced the commander-in-chief to entrust its conduct to him. There is no doubt that the intention of the enemy was to enter the harbor at night, and in the surprise seize the shipping and forts, make the garrisons prisoners, and after making themselves masters of the town, load their transports with the rich plunder, and dispatch them with the captured vessels to New York.

All this the enemy reasonably supposed could be accomplished; the sloops-of-war brought before the town, and the forts garrisoned by British soldiers, before the alarm could be given by the inhabitants. When once in possession the holding of the forts and town by these disciplined troops, with their facilities for communicating with New York, against the un-trained militia, would be a matter of comparative ease. In case the cap-ture did not recall Washington, a safe base from which to make an inva-sion of New England would be secured. On the afternoon of the 4th the fleet of transports and sloops-of-war, under command of Captain Beazley in the Amphion, weighed anchor, and under easy sail proceeded with a fair wind down the Sound toward its objective point. On the following day, the 5th, at two P. M., it came to anchor under Long Isl-and shore, directly across from and within about thirty miles of New London. The reason of this delay was to avoid appearing off New London before darkness should cover their approach. Thus far all had apparently tended to the enemy's advantage, but now they miscalculated on the continuance of the wind in their favor. Along the New England coast during the summer and early autumn—with a regularity almost unbroken, except by storms—the wind, soon after twelve o'clock M., commences to blow from the south and west; this continues gradually decreasing in force until at about three o'clock in the morning, when, after a short period of rest, (like the turning of the tide,) it begins to blow from the north and west, in which direction it continues until at not far from eleven A. M., when it is succeeded by a calm, followed by a southerly breeze.

The British officers calculated on this south wind continuing as usual, so that by availing themselves of it to be able to arrive off the town at from about midnight to an hour later. They accordingly weighed anchor at 7 P. M., not doubting that the five or six miles an hour required to reach New London by the appointed time would be easily accomplished.

In this they were disappointed. The south wind died away and was succeeded by that from the north nearly two hours earlier than usual, so that by beating the fleet was just able to arrive at the mouth of the harbor at 9 o'clock in the morning—some four or five hours after it had been observed from the forts, and its approach heralded to the startled country by the alarm guns. As soon as the hostile intentions of the enemy were manifest, Colonel Ledyard repaired to New London and dispatched expresses to Governor Trumbull at Lebanon, and the various militia commanders in the neighboring towns apprising them of his danger, and soliciting aid in making a stand in defence of their homes and the honor of their country. He then re-crossed the river to Fort Griswold, and prepared, so far as his limited means would allow, to meet the storm which he saw was inevitable.   *   *   *   *   We have now arrived at the point in the history of that eventful day at which begins the graphic description of its bloody scenes by participants. As it is no part of the plan of this work to give a new version of the battle, but rather to preserve the old, these introductory remarks properly close here, and give place to the story as related by eye-witnesses and their cotemporaries.

AN ACCOUNT

OF THE

BURNING OF NEW LONDON,

ON THE

6TH OF SEPTEMBER, 1781.

From the Connecticut Gazette of Friday, September 7th.

AT about day-break on Thursday morning last, twenty-four sail of the enemy's shipping appeared to the westward of this harbour, which by many were supposed to be a plundering party after stock.

Alarm guns were immediately fired, but the discharge of cannon in the harbour has become so frequent of late that they answered little or no purpose.[1] The defenceless state of the fortifications and town are obvious to our readers. A few of the inhabitants who were equipped advanced toward the place where the enemy were tho't likely to make their landing, and manœuvred on the heights adjacent, until the enemy, about 9 o'clk, landed in two divisions of about 800 men each, one of them at Brown's farm near the light-house, the other at Groton point. The division

---

[1] During the war the privateers which swarmed from New London were in the habit of announcing their successes on their return to port by firing salutes from their guns. Colonel Samuel McClellan, of Woodstock, (great-grandfather of General G. B. McClellan,) who, after the death of Colonel Ledyard, assumed command of New London harbor and its defences soon after the battle, forbade the firing of guns in the harbor, except in hostilities with the enemy.

2

that landed near the light-house marched up the road, keep-
ing out large flanking parties, who were attacked in different places on their march by the inhabitants who had spirit
and resolution to oppose their progress; the main body of
the enemy proceeded to the town and set fire to the stores
on the beach,[1] and immediately after to the dwelling-houses
lying on the Mill Cove. The scattered fire of our little
parties unsupported by our neighbours more distant galled
them, so that they soon began to retire, setting fire to stores
and dwelling-houses promiscuously in their way; the fire
from the stores communicated to the shipping that lay at
the wharfs, and a number were burnt; others swung to single fasts and remained unburnt. At 4 o'clk they began to
quit the town with great precipitation, and were pursued by
our brave citizens with the spirit of veterans and drove on
board their boats. Five of the enemy were killed and about
20 wounded. Among the latter is a Hessian captain, who
is a prisoner, as are seven others. We lost four killed and
ten or twelve wounded—none mortal. The most valuable
part of the town is reduced to ashes, and all the stores.
Fort Trumbull not being tenable on the land side, was
evacuated as the enemy advanced, and the few men in it
crossed the river to Fort Griswold, on Groton Hill, which
was soon after invested by the division that landed on the
point. The fort having in it only 120 men, chiefly militia,
hastily collected, who defended it with the greatest resolution and bravery, and once repulsed the enemy, but the fort
being out of repair could not be defended by such a handful of men, th° brave and determined, against so superior
a number, they did ALL that men of spirit and bravery in
such a situation could do; but after having a number of

---

[1] What was then known as "the beach" is now Water Street. It at
that time was the business part of the town. On it were the public and
large private store-houses.

their party killed and wounded they found that further resistance would be in vain, and resigned the fort. Immediately on their surrendery the valient Colonel Ledyard, whose
fate in a particular manner is much lamented, and 70
other officers and men were murdered, most of them heads
of families. The enemy lost a Major Montgomery and
forty-one officers and men in the attack, who were found
near the fort; their wounded were carried off. Soon after
the enemy got possession of the fort they set fire to and
burnt a number of dwelling-houses and stores on Groton
bank, and embarked about sunset, taking with them sundry
of the inhabitants of New London and Groton. A Colonel
Ayres,[1] who commanded the division, was wounded, and it
is said died on board the fleet the night they embarked.

About 15 sail of vessels with effects of the inhabitants
retreated up the river on the approach of the enemy, and
were saved, and four others remained in the harbor unhurt.
The troops were commanded by that infamous traitor to
his country, Benedict Arnold, who headed the division
which proceded to the town. By this calamity it is judged
that more than one hundred families are deprived of their
habitations, and most of them their **ALL**. This neighborhood feel sensibly the loss of many deserving citizens, and,
th° deceased, can⁵ᵗ but be highly indebted to them for their
spirit and bravery in their exertions and manly opposition to
the merciless enemies of our country in their last moments.

From the same Paper of September 14*th*, 1781.

The following savage action, committed by the troops
who subdued Fort Griswold on Groton hill, on Thursday
last, ought to be accorded to their eternal infamy:

Soon after the surrendery of the fort they loaded a wagon
with our wounded men, by orders of their officers, and set

---

[1] Eyre.

the wagon off from the top of the hill, which is long and very steep; the wagon went a considerable distance with great force, till it was suddenly stopped by a tree; the shock was so great to those faint and bleeding men that part of them died instantly; the officers ordered their men to fire on the wagon while it was running. By the best information we can get there were six killed and 20 wounded previous to the enemy's gaining possession of the fort. The number of the enemy found buried in Groton amounts to 61. The whole number of killed, including those who have since died of their wounds, is said to be 82.

The following is a list of dwelling-houses, stores, &c., in New London which were set on fire by the enemy and consumed:

On the north end of Main Street.

	No. of Families.
Picket Latimer's house and barn, - - -	1
Widow Plumbe's house and barn, - -	2
Henry Latimer's (late) house, - - -	1
Late Deacon Green's house and shop, - -	4
Christopher Prince's house, - - - -	1
James Pitman's house, - - - -	1
Daniel Byrne's house, - - - -	1
Roswell Saltonstall's house and cooper's shop, -	1
Joseph Hurlbut's house and cooper's shop, - -	1
Widow Rogers's house, - - -	1
Henry Deshon's house, - - - -	1
Gen. Saltonstall's house, 2 stores, shop and barn, -	1
Store improved by Owen Neil for a house, - -	1
Late Duncan Stewart's house, - - -	2
Heirs of Peter Harris, 1 store and one barn.	
Joseph Packwood's store.	
Roger Gibson's house, - - - -	2
Samuel and Richard Latimer's house, - -	2

No. of Families.

Ichabod Powers's house, - - -	2
Peter Latimer's house and cooper's shop, - -	4
Widow Shapley's house, - - -	1

Guy Richards & Son, 3 stores and slaughter house.

John Hartell's work-shop.

On Beach Street.[1]

Widow Elliot's house and barn, - -	2

Edward Hallam & Co., 3 stores and barn.

David Mumford's store.

Roswell Saltonstall's distill, house and store.

do do opposite thereto 1 store and a cooper's shop improv'd as a house, - - -	1
Store improv'd by John Springer's family, - -	1

Thomas Wilson's store.

Shoe-maker's shop.

Nathaniel Shaw's two stores.

Joseph Packwood's store.

John Deshon's house and two stores, - -	1
Widow Skinner's house, - - -	1
Elijah Richards's house, - - - -	1
Widow Potter's house, - - - -	2
Barsheba Smith's house, - - - -	2
Court house, church, jail, jail-house, watch-house and barber's shop, - - - - -	2

On the Bank.[2]

Samuel Belden's store.

do do do on the wharf improv'd by a family,	1

---

[1] When the enemy, passing down Main Street, came to Hallam Street, through which they entered Water Street, Arnold is said to have exclaimed, pointing with his sword in the direction of the street with its rich stores, "Soldiers, do your duty!"

[2] Now known as Bank Street.

No. of Families.

Widow Hancock's two houses, - - -	2
Shop improv'd by Thomas Gardiner.	
John Erving's house, one store and barn, - -	1
Jonathan Douglass's house and cooper's shop, -	1
Daniel Deshon's house, - - - -	3
Widow Leete's house, - - - -	1
Charles Chadwick's house and empty store, - -	1
John Champlin's shop.	
James Thomson's house and barn, - - -	2
Samuel Belden's house and barn, - -	1
John M'Curdy's house, 2 stores, and barn, - -	1
Widow M'Neil's house, and shop opposite, -	1
Richard Potter's house and store, - - -	1
Widow Bulkley's two houses, - - -	4
Widow Fosdick's house and barn, - - -	1
Jonathan Starr's work-shop.	
Jere. Miller's house, store, and barn, - -	1
Joshua Starr's house and work-shop, - -	2
do do do and barn, - - -	1
Titus Hurlbut's 2 houses, 2 shops, and barn, -	5
James Tilley's house, rope-walk, and barn, - -	1
Doct. Walcott's house and barn, - -	1
Jacob Fink's house and slaughter house, - -	1
John Way's house and cooper shop, - -	1
Russel Hubbard's house, store, and barn, - -	3
James Lamphear's house, - - -	2
Widow Short's house, - - - -	4
Andrew Palmes's house, - - -	2
Nathan Douglas's house, tan-house, and barn, -	1
Jere. Miller's house improved by W. Constant, -	1
Joseph Coit's house and two barns, - - -	1
do do on the wharf, one house and two stores, .	1
Nath'l Shaw's house, shop, and two stores, -	3

At the head of Long Bridge Cove.[1]

No. of Families.

Deshon & Christopher's house and tan-house, - 1

A house on Hog Neck,[2] - - - - 1

Total, 65 houses containing 97 families, 31 stores, 18 shops, 20 barns, 9 public and other buildings, besides a variety of other small buildings of different kinds not here enumerated.

Total of buildings here inumerated, - - 143

There were burnt at Groton at the same time 1 school-house, 4 barns, 2 shops, 2 stores, and 12 dwelling-houses.

From the same paper of September 21st, 1781.

Since our last 7 or 8 dead bodies of officers and soldiers have drove ashore on the Great Neck, and 3 others on Groton shore which were thrown out of Arnold's burning fleet. Our advices from New York are, that the enemy lost 220 men, killed and dead of their wounds, in their attack on Groton Fort and this place, besides about 70 deserters.

The following is the most accurate list we have been able to collect of the names of the brave and worthy citizens who were murdered at Fort Griswold Sept. 6, 1781, including those who have since died of their wounds.

The whole number of killed and those since died of their wounds is said to be 82. Should we be able to collect the names of the others, they shall be published.

---

[1] Now Truman, Blinman, and Coit Streets.
[2] Howard Street.

BELONGING TO GROTON.

Lieut.-Col. William Ledyard, Mess. Luke Perkins,
Mess. Elijah Avery, Capt.,

John Williams,
Simeon Allen,
Samuel Allen,
Amos Stanton,
Hubbart Burrows,
Nathan Moor,
Youngs Ledyard,
Joseph Lewis,
Henry Williams,
Ebenezer Avery,
John Lester,
John Stedman,
Daniel Avery,
David Avery, Esq.,
Daniel Chester,
Solomon Avery,
Jasper Avery,
Elisha Avery,
Thomas Avery,
David Palmer,
Sylvester Walworth,
Philip Covil,
Ezekiel Bailey,
Jeremiah Chester,
Daniel Seabury,
Henry Woodbridge,
Christopher Woodbridge,
Elnathan Perkins,

Luke Perkins, Jun.,
Elisha Perkins,
Asa Perkins,
Simeon Perkins,
John Brown,
John P. Babcock,
Nathaniel Adams,
Barney Kinne,
Samuel Hill,
Nathan Shales,
Joseph Moxley,
Thomas Starr, Jun.,
Nicholas Starr,
Moses Jones,
Rufus Hurlbut,
Belton Allen,
Benadam Allen,
Andrew Billings,
Simeon Morgan,
Patrick Ward,
Christopher Avery,
Jonas Lester,
Edward Mills,
Wait Lester,
Thomas Miner,
Andrew Baker,
Solomon Tift,
Josiah Wigger.

BELONGING TO NEW LONDON.

Mess. Peter Richards,
James Comstock,
Richard Chapman,
John Holt,
Samuel Billings,
John Clark,
John Whittelsey,

Mess. Stephen Whittelsey,
Eliaday Jones,
Jonathan Butler,
Wm. Comstock, of
Fort Trumbull,
Daniel Williams,
William Bolton.

BELONGING TO STONINGTON.

Mess. Enoch Stanton,
Thomas Williams,

Daniel Stanton.

BELONGING TO PRESTON.
Mr. John Billings.

BELONGING TO LONG ISLAND.
Capt. Ellis,   Henry Halsey.

Negroes.—Lambo Latham, Jordan Freeman.

3

NARRATIVE

OF

RUFUS AVERY,

Containing an account of the transactions at New London and Groton, on the 6th September, 1781, in his own words.

I HAD charge of the garrison the night previous to the attack. The enemy had not yet appeared near us, nor did we expect them at this time more than ever; but it is true "we know not what shall be on the morrow." About 3 o'clock in the morning, as soon as daylight appeared, so as I could look off, I saw the fleet in the harbor, a little distance below the light house; it consisted of thirty-two in number, ships, brigs, schooners and sloops. It may well be imagined that a shock of consternation, and a thrill of dread apprehension flashed over me. I immediately sent for Captain William Latham, who was captain of said fort, and who was near by. He came and saw the fleet, and sent notice to Colonel Ledyard, who was commander of the harbor, and also of Forts Griswold and Trumbull. He ordered two large guns to be loaded with heavy charges of good powder, &c. Captain William Latham took charge of the one which was to be discharged from the north east part of the fort, and I had to attend the other, on the west side, and thus we as speedily as possible prepared to give alarm to the vicinity, as was to be expected in case of danger, two guns being the specified signal for alarm in distress. But a difficulty now arose from having all our plans communicated by a traitor! The enemy understood our signal was two regular guns, and they fired a third, which broke our alarm, and caused it to signify good news or a prize, and thus it was understood by our troops, and several companies which were lying back ready to come to our assistance in case of necessity were by this measure deterred from coming. The reader may well suppose, though time would not permit us to consider, or anticipate long, yet the sense of our helplessness without additional strength, and arms, was dreadful; but the trying events of the few coming hours we had not known! Colonel Ledyard now sent expresses from both forts, to call on every militia captain to hurry with their companies to the forts. But few came; their excuse was, that it was but a false alarm, or for some trifling alarm. The enemy's boats now approached and landed eight hundred officers and men, some horses, carriages and cannon, on the Groton side of the river, about 8 o'clock in the morning; and another division on the New London side, below the light house, consisting of about seven hundred officers and men. The army on Groton banks was divided into two divisions. Colonel Ayres took command of the division south east of the forts, consisting of about half, sheltering them behind a ledge of rocks, about one hundred and thirty rods back. Major Montgomery with his division about one hundred and fifty rods from the fort, behind a high hill. The army on New London side of the river, had better and more accommodating land to march on than that on Groton side. As soon as their army had got opposite Fort Trumbull, they divided, and one part proceeded to the city of New London, plundered and set fire to the shipping and buildings, the rest marched down to Fort Trumbull. Captain Adam Shapley, who commanded, seeing that he was likely to be overpowered by the enemy, spiked his cannon, and embarked on board the boats which had been prepared for him in case of necessity; but the enemy were so quick upon him, that before he and his little handful of men could get out of the reach of their guns, seven men were badly wounded in the boats. The remaining one reached Fort Griswold, where, poor fellows, they met a mortal blow.

Ayres and Montgomery got their army stationed about 9 o'clock in the morning. When they appeared in sight we threw a number of shots among them, but they would immediately contrive to disappear behind their hills. About 10 o'clock they sent a flag of truce to demand the surrender of the fort. When the flag was within about forty rods from the fort, we sent a musket ball in front of them, and brought them to a stand. Colonel Ledyard called a council of war, to ascertain the minds of his officers and friends about what was best to be done in this momentous hour, when every moment indicated a bloody and decisive battle. They all agreed in council to send a flag to them. They did so, choosing Captain Elijah Avery, Captain Amos Staunton,[1] and Captain John Williams, who went immediately to meet the British flag and receive their demand, which was to give up the fort to them. The council was then inquired of what was to be done? and the answer returned to the British flag was, that "the fort would not be given up to the British." The flag then returned to their division commanded by Ayres, but soon returned to us again; when about a proper distance our flag met them and attended to their summons, and came back to inform Colonel Ledyard, that the enemy declared that "if they were obliged to take

---

[1] Captain Staunton, a man of almost gigantic stature and herculean strength, on seeing the slaughter continued after the surrender, is said to have seized a heavy musket by the muzzle, and exclaiming "My God, must we die so!" sprang upon the platform on the west side of the fort, and nearly cleared it of the enemy before he was brought down by a musket shot.

it by storm, they should put the Martial Law in full force," that is, "what they did not kill by ball they should put to death by sword and bayonet!" Colonel Ledyard sent back the decisive answer, that "we should not give up the fort to them, let the consequences be what they would."

While these flags were passing and repassing, we were exchanging shots with the British at Fort Trumbull, as they had got possession of it before the battle commenced in action at Fort Griswold. We could throw our shot into Fort Trumbull without any difficulty, but the British could not cause theirs to enter Fort Griswold, because they could not aim high enough. They had got possession and in use, some of our best pieces and ammunition, which were left in Fort Trumbull when Captain Shapley left it and retreated. About 11 o'clock in the morning, when they perceived what we were about to do, they started with both their divisions, Colonel Ayres advancing with his in solid columns. As soon as they reached the level ground, and in a proper range, we saluted them with an eighteen pounder, then loaded with two bags of grape shot. Captain Elias H. Halsey was the one who directed the guns, and took aim at the enemy. He had long practiced on board a privateer, and manifested his skill at this time. I was at the gun with others when it was discharged into the British ranks, and it cleared a very wide space in their solid columns. It has been reported, by good authority, that about twenty were killed and wounded by that one discharge of grape shot. As soon as the column was broken by loss of men and officers, they were seen to scatter and trail arms, coming on with a quick step towards the fort, inclining to the west. We continued firing, but they advanced upon the south and west side of the fort. Colonel Ayres was mortally wounded. Major Montgomery now advanced with his division, coming on in solid columns, bearing around to the north, until they got east of the redoubt or battery, which was east of the fort, then marching with a quick step into the battery.   Here we sent among them large and repeated charges of grape shot, which destroyed a number, as we could perceive them thinned and broken.   Then they started for the fort, a part of them in platoons, discharging their guns; and some of the officers and men scattering, they came around on the east and north side of the fort. Here Major Montgomery fell, near the north east part of the fort.   We might suppose the loss of their commanders might have dismayed them, but they had proceeded so far, and the excitement and determination on slaughter was so great, they could not be prevented.   As soon as their army had entirely surrounded the garrison, a man attempted to open the gates, but he lost his life in a moment before he could succeed.   There was hard fighting, and shocking slaughter, and much blood spilt before another attempt was made to open the gates, which was at this time successful; for our little number, which was only one hundred and fifty-five, officers and privates, (the most of them volunteers,) were by this time overpowered.   There was then no block house on the parade as there is now, so that the enemy had every chance to wound and kill every man.   When they had overpowered us and driven us from our station at the breastwork into the fort, and Colonel Ledyard saw how few men he had remaining to fight with, he ceased resistance. They all left their posts and went on to the open parade in the fort, where the enemy had a fair opportunity to massacre us, as there were only six of us to an hundred of them! This, this was a moment of indescribable misery!   We can fight with good hearts while *hope* and prospects of victory aid us; but, after we have fought and bled, and availed nothing, to yield to be massacred by the boasting enemy, "tries men's hearts!"   Our ground was drenched with human gore; our wounded and dying could not have any attendance, while each man was almost hopeless of his own preservation; but our country's danger caused the most acute anxiety. Now I saw the enemy mount the parapets like so many madmen, all at once seemingly. They swung their hats around, and then discharged their guns into the fort, and then those who had not fallen by ball they began to massacre with sword and bayonet. I was on the west side of the fort, with Captain Edward Latham and Mr. C. Latham, standing on the platform, and had a full view of the enemy's conduct. I had then a hole through my clothes by a ball, and a bayonet rent through my coat to my flesh. The enemy approached us, knocked down the two men I mentioned, with the britch of their guns, and I expected had ended their lives, but they did not. By this time that division which had been commanded by Montgomery, now under charge of Bloomfield, unbolted the other gates, marched into the fort and formed into a solid column. I at this moment left my station and went across the parade, towards the south end of the barracks. I noticed Colonel William Ledyard on the parade stepping towards the enemy and Bloomfield, gently raising and lowering his sword as a token of bowing and submission; he was about six feet from them when I turned my eyes off from him, and went up to the door of the barracks and looked at the enemy who were discharging their guns through the windows. It was but a moment that I had turned my eyes from Colonel Ledyard and saw him alive, and now I saw him weltering in his gore![1] Oh the hellish spite and madness of a man

---

[1] The chivalrous Ledyard seems to have felt a premonition of impending calamity from the beginning. On stepping into the boat to cross from New London on the morning, he remarked to friends gathered about him, "If I have this day to lose either life or honor, you who know me best know which it will be."

that will murder a reasonable and noble-hearted officer in the act of submitting and surrendering! I can assure my countrymen that I felt the thrill of such a horrid deed, more than the honorable and martial-like war of months! We are informed that the wretch who murdered him exclaimed, as he came near, "Who commands this fort?" Ledyard handsomely replied, "I did, but *you* do now;" at the same moment handing him his sword, which the unfeeling villian buried in his breast.[1] The column continued

---

[1]. Since this transaction there has ever existed in the public mind great uncertainty as to *who* was the murderer of Colonel Ledyard, the odium being divided between Major Bromfield, who succeeded Major Montgomery in command of the British troops on that occasion, and Captain Beckwith, of the 54th regiment. No person who actually witnessed the deed survived the battle, or if any did they left no account of it behind them, and therefore the version of the manner of Ledyard's death, commonly received as the correct one, is but merely a conjecture at the most. By this, the deed is ascribed to the officer who received Ledyard's surrender of the fort, supposed by the greater number to have been Major Bromfield; others at the time, and for a long time subsequent, laid the infamous transaction to the charge of Captain Beckwith, supposing him to have been the officer who met Ledyard and demanded the surrender.

Let us consider the matter a little, and see if we be able to reconcile the known facts and strong probabilities in the case with this generally received opinion. Upon the entry of the British officer to the fort, and at his demand of who commanded it, Colonel Ledyard advanced to answer "I did," &c., at the same time tendering him the hilt of his sword in token of submission. It is obvious that in this action Colonel Ledyard must have presented the front of his person to that officer. Now had the latter, in taking the surrendered sword, instantly (as all accounts charge him with having done) plunged it into him, is it not also evident that it must have entered in front and passed out of the back of his person? The vest and shirt worn that day by Colonel Ledyard, preserved in the Wadsworth Athenæum at Hartford, upon examination reveal two rough, jagged openings, one on either side, a little before and in a line with the lower edge of the arm-holes of the vest. The larger of these apertures is upon the left side; the difference in size between it and that on the right corresponds with the taper of a sabre blade from hilt to point, showing conclusively that the weapon entered from the left and

marching towards the south end of the parade, and I could
do no better than to go across the parade before them amid

passed out at the right, and that the person by whom the wound was inflicted must have stood upon the left side of the wearer when the plunge
was made.   These holes are marked—that on the left, as "where the
sword entered," and that on the right, as "where the sword came out"
—so marked, doubtless, by the person who presented these memorials to
the society, a near relative of Colonel Ledyard, and who considered them
as the marks of the fatal wound.   These are the only marks visible upon
the garment.   It is a reasonable supposition that when the British officer
entered and thundered his demand, he carried his drawn sword in his
right hand, for we can scarcely imagine an officer rushing unarmed into
a place of such danger and demanding a surrender.   Now in case he
did so carry his sword, he must necessarily either have sheathed, dropped,
or changed it to his left hand, in order to receive Ledyard's with the
right; and this hardly seems possible.   We must therefore suppose that
he received it in his left hand; and if so, does it not appear as most un-
reasonable that having a sword in either hand, he would have used that
in his left with which to make the thrust? yet he must have done so if
it was by *his own sword* that Ledyard met his death.   Neither does it
appear possible that in the heat and excitement of the engagement—
coolly calculating the chances—he would have passed around to the left
of his victim for the purpose of making the wound more surely fatal—
the only reason for which we can suppose it to have been done.

   We have seen from the position occupied by the parties that the
wound, if inflicted instantly on the surrender of the sword, must have
been given in front—the marks in the vest conclusively prove it to have
been given in the left side.   We have seen the awkward position of the
officer with his own sword in his right and Ledyard's in his left hand—a
situation almost precluding the idea of his making the stab with the latter.
We have also seen that no person who witnessed it left any testimony
regarding the affair, and that all that the commonly received version of
it is based upon is really but the surmises of a people wrought almost to
desperation by their losses and wrongs, who in the first moments of ex-
asperation would naturally attribute an act of such enormity to the commander as the representative of the enemy.   Now after considering all
these facts and probabilities, is it not a more rational conclusion that the
wound was given by a bystanding officer—a subaltern or aid perhaps—
than that it was inflicted by the officer to whom Ledyard offered his
sword?   It certainly so appears to us.   But in case that, despite all these

4

their fire.   They discharged three platoons as I crossed before them at this time.   I believe there were not less than five or six hundred of the British on the parade and in the fort.   They killed and wounded every man they possibly could, and it was all done in less than two minutes!   I had nothing to expect but to drop with the rest; one mad looking fellow put his bayonet to my side, swearing "by Jesus he would skipper me!"   I looked him earnestly in the face and eyes, and begged him to have mercy and spare my

---

reasons for believing that officer innocent of the crime, he was really guilty, of the two to whom it has been charged, against but one is there any evidence to sustain the charge, and this is purely circumstantial.   Captain Beckwith acted as aid to Lieutenant-Colonel Eyre on the day of the battle, and was the officer sent to demand the surrender of the fort.   He, with Lord Dalrymple, was sent by Arnold as bearer of dispatches to Sir Henry Clinton, and in all probability furnished the account of the battle for Rivington's Gazette, *which appeared in that paper before the remainder of the expedition had reached New York.*   In this account, in which the details of the conference regarding the surrender are given with a minuteness with which only an eye-witness could give them, personal malice toward Colonel Ledyard is a salient feature, which the most unobservant reader can not fail to notice.   The writer appears to have considered the flag, and the officers bearing it, insulted in the conference; and in his references to the garrison, and to Colonel Ledyard in particular, he expresses himself in the most contemptuous and bitter terms.

If he was the officer to whom the surrender was made, it is possible that on beholding the man who he fancied had insulted him, he allowed his rage to supplant his manhood, and, forgetting his military honor, plunged his sword into his vanquished enemy.   From Miss Caulkins' History of New London we learn that he afterward passed through New York on his way to Barbadoes.   While there he was charged by the newspapers of that city with the murder, which he indignantly denied.   A correspondence was opened between him and a relative of Colonel Ledyard in reference to the question, when he produced documents which exculpated him.   In view of this, however, as between him and Major Bromfield, circumstantial evidence is strongly in favor of the latter, who doubtless could have furnished as full documentary proof of his innocence had he been called upon for it.

life! I must say I believe God prevented him from killing me, for he put his bayonet three times into me, and I seemed to be in his power, as well as Lieutenant Enoch Staunton, who was stabbed to the heart and fell at my feet at this time. I think no scene ever exceeded this for *continued* and barbarous massacre after surrender. There were two large doors to the magazine, which made a space wide enough to admit ten men to stand in one rank. There marched up a platoon of ten men just by where I stood, and at once discharged their guns into the magazine among our killed and wounded, and also among those who had escaped uninjured, and as soon as these had fired another platoon was ready, and immediately took their place when they fell back. At this moment Bloomfield came swiftly around the corner of the building, and raising his sword with exceeding quickness exclaimed, "stop firing, or you will send us all to *hell* together!" I was very near him when he spoke. He knew there must be much powder deposited and scattered about the magazine, and if they continued throwing in fire we should all be blown up. I think it must, before this, have been the case, had not the ground and every thing been wet with human blood. We trod in blood! We trampled under feet the limbs of our countrymen, our neighbors and dear kindred. Our ears were filled with the groans of the dying, when the more stunning sound of the artillery would give place to the death shrieks. After this they ceased killing and went to stripping, not only the dead, but the wounded and those who were not wounded. They then ordered us all who were able to march, to the northeast part of the parade, and those who could walk to help those who were wounded so bad as not to go of themselves. Mr. Samuel Edgcomb, Jr., and myself were ordered to carry out Ensign Charles E'dridge, who was shot through the knee joints; he was a

very large, heavy man, and with our fasting and violent
exercise of the day, we were but ill able to do it, or more
than to sustain our own weight; but we had to submit.
We with all the prisoners were taken out upon the parade,
about two rods from the fort, and ordered to sit down immediately, or they would put their bayonets into us. The
battle was now ended. It was about 1 o'clock in the afternoon, and since the hour of eight in the morning, what a
scene of carnage, of anxiety, and of loss had we experienced. The enemy now began to take care of their dead
and wounded. They took off six of the outer doors of
the barracks, and with four men at each door, they brought
in one man at a time. There were twenty-four men thus
employed for two hours, as fast as they could walk. They
deposited them on the west side of the parade, in the fort,
where it was the most comfortable place, and screened from
the hot sun which was pouring down upon us, aggravating
our wounds, and causing many to faint and die who might
have lived with good care. By my side lay two most
worthy and excellent officers, Captain Youngs Ledyard
and Captain N. Moore, in the agonies of death. Their
heads rested on my thighs as I sat or lay there. They had
their reason well and spoke. They asked for water. I
could give them none, as I was to be thrust through if I
got up. I asked the enemy, who were passing by us, to
give us some water for my dying friends and for myself.
As the well was near they granted this request; but even
then I feared they would put something poison into it, that
they might get us out of the way the sooner; and they had
said repeatedly that the last of us should die before the
sun set! Oh what revenge and inhumanity pervaded their
steeled hearts! They effected what was threatened in the
summons, sent by the flag in the morning, to Colonel Ledyard, "That those who were not killed by the musket

should be by the sword," &c. But I must think they became tired of human butchery, and so let us live. They
kept us the ground, the garrison charged, till about two
hours had been spent in taking care of their men, and then
came and ordered every man of us that could walk to "rise
up." Sentries were placed around with guns loaded and
bayonets fixed, and orders given that every one who would
not, in a moment, obey commands, should be shot dead or
run through! I had to leave the two dying men who were
resting on me, dropping their heads on the cold and hard
ground, giving them one last and pitying look. Oh God,
this was hard work. They both died that night. We
marched down to the bank of the river so as to be ready
to embark on board the British vessels. There were about
thirty of us surrounded by sentries. Captain Bloomfield
then came and took down the names of the prisoners who
were able to march down with us. Where I sat I had a
fair view of their movements. They were setting fire to
the buildings, and bringing the plunder and laying it down
near us. The sun was about half an hour high. I can
never forget the whole appearance of all about me. New
London was in flames. The inhabitants deserted their habitations to save life, which was more highly prized. Above
and around us were our unburied dead and our dying
friends. None to appeal to for sustenance in our exhausted
state but a maddened enemy—not allowed to move a step
or make any resistance, but with loss of life—and sitting to
see the property of our neighbors consumed by fire, or the
spoils of a triumphing enemy!

Reader, but little can be described, while much is felt.
There were still remaining, near the fort, a great number of
the British who were getting ready to leave. They loaded
up our large ammunition wagon that belonged to the fort
with the wounded men that could not walk, and about

twenty of the enemy drew it from the fort to the brow of
the hill which leads down to the river. The declivity is
very steep for the distance of thirty rods to the river. As
soon as the wagon began to move down the hill, it pressed
so hard against them that they found they were unable to
hold it back, and jumped away from it as quick as possible,
leaving it to thrash along down the hill with great speed,
till the shafts struck a large apple-tree stump with a most
violent crash, hurting the poor dying and wounded men in
it in a most inhuman manner. Some of the wounded fell
out and fainted away; then a part of the company where
I sat ran and brought the men and the wagon along. They
by some means got the prisoners who were wounded badly,
into a house near by, belonging to Ensign Ebenezer Avery,
who was one of the wounded in the wagon. Before the
prisoners were brought to the house the soldiers had set fire
to it, but others put it out, and made use of it for this purpose. Captain Bloomfield paroled, to be left at home here,
these wounded prisoners, and took Ebenezer Ledyard, Esq.,
as hostage for them, to see them forthcoming when called
for. Now the boats had come for us who could go on
board the fleet. The officer spoke with a doleful and me-
nacing tone, "Come, you rebels, go on board." This was
a consummation of all I had seen or endured through the
day. This wounded my feelings in a thrilling manner.
After all my sufferings and toil, to add the pang of leaving
my native land, my wife, my good neighbors, and probably
to suffer still more with cold and hunger, for already I had
learned that I was with a cruel enemy. But I was in the
hands of a higher power, over which no human being could
hold superior control, and by God's preservation I am still
alive, through all the hardships and dangers of the war,
while almost every one about me, who shared the same,
has met either a natural or an unnatural death. When we,

the prisoners, went down to the shore to the boats, they would not bring them near, but kept them off where the water was knee deep to us, obliging us, weak and worn as we were, to wade to them. We were marched down in two ranks, one on each side of the boat. The officer spoke very harshly to us, to "get aboard immediately." They rowed us down to an armed sloop, commanded by one Captain Thomas, as they called him, a refugee tory, and he lay with his vessel within the fleet. As soon as we were on board they hurried us down into the hold of the sloop, where were their fires for cooking, and besides being very hot, it was filled with smoke. The hatch-way was closed tight, so that we were near suffocating for want of air to breathe. We begged them to spare our lives, so they gave us some relief, by opening the hatch-way and permitting us to come upon deck by two or three at a time, but not without sentries watching us with gun and bayonet. We were now extremely exhausted and faint for want of food, when, after being on board twenty-four hours, they gave us a mess of *hogs' brains*—the hogs which they took on Groton banks when they plundered there. After being on board Thomas's sloop nearly three days, with nothing to eat or drink that we could swallow, we began to feel as if a struggle must be made, in some way, to prolong our existence, which, after all our escapes, seemed still to be depending. In such a time we can know for a reality how strong is the love of life. In the room where we were confined were a great many weapons of war, and some of the prisoners whispered that we might make a prize of the sloop. This in some way was overheard, and got to the officer's ears, and now we were immediately put in a stronger place in the hold of the vessel; and they appeared so enraged that I was almost sure we should share a decisive fate, or suffer severely. Soon they commenced calling us, one by one, on deck. As I went up they seized me, tied my hands behind me with a strong rope-yarn, and drew it so tight that my shoulder-bones cracked, and almost touched each other. Then a boat came from a fourteen-gun brig, commanded by one Steele. Into this boat I was ordered to get, without the use of my hands, over the sloop's bulwarks, which were all of three feet high, and then from these I had to fall, or throw myself into the boat. My distress of body and agitated feelings I can not describe; and no relief could be anticipated, but only forebodings of a more severe fate. A prisoner with an enemy, an enraged and revengeful enemy, is a place where I pray my reader may never come. They made us all lie down under the seats on which the man sat to row, and so we were conveyed to the brig; going on board, we were ordered to stand in one rank by the gunwale, and in front of us was placed a spar within about a foot of each man. Here we stood, with a sentry to each of us, having orders to shoot or bayonet us if we attempted to stir out of our place. All this time we had nothing to eat or drink, and it rained and was very cold. We were detained in this position about two hours, when we had liberty to go about the main deck. Night approached, and we had no supper, nor any thing to lie upon but the wet deck. We were on board this brig about four days, and then were removed on board a ship commanded by Captain Scott, who was very kind to the prisoners. He took me on to the quarter deck with him, and appeared to have the heart of a man. I should think he was about sixty years of age. I remained with him until I was exchanged. Captain Nathaniel Shaw came down to New York with the American flag, after me and four others, who were prisoners with me, and belonged to Fort Griswold, and who were brave and fine young men. General Mifflin went with the British flag to meet this American flag. I sailed with him about twenty miles. He asked me many questions, all of which I took caution how I answered, and gave him no information. I told him I was very sorry that he should come to destroy so many, many brave men, burn their property, distress so many families, and make such desolation. I did not think they could be said to be honorable in so doing. He said "we might thank our own countrymen for it." I told him I had no thanks for him. I then asked the general if I might ask him a few questions. "As many as you please." I asked him how many of the army who made the attack upon New London and Groton were missing. As you, sir, are the commissary of the British army, I suppose you can tell. He replied, "that by the returns there were two hundred and twenty odd missing, but what had become of them he knew not." We advanced, and the flags met, and I was exchanged and permitted to return home. Here I close my narrative; for, as I was requested, I have given a particular and unexaggerated account of that which I saw with mine own eyes.

RUFUS AVERY,
Orderly Sergeant under Captain William Latham.

5

NARRATIVE

OF

STEPHEN HEMPSTEAD.

ON the morning of the 6th of September, 1781, twenty-four sail of the enemy's shipping appeared to the westward of New London harbor. The enemy landed in two divisions, of about 800 men each, commanded by that infamous traitor to his country, Benedict Arnold, who headed the division that landed on the New London side, near Brown's farms; the other division, commanded by Colonel Ayres, landed on Groton Point, nearly opposite. I was first sergeant of Captain Adam Shapley's company of state troops, and was stationed with him at the time, with about twenty-three men, at Fort Trumbull, on the New London side. This was a mere breast-work or water battery, open from behind, and the enemy coming on us from that quarter, we spiked our cannon, and commenced a retreat across the river to Fort Griswold in three boats. The enemy was so near that they over-shot us with their muskets, and succeeded in capturing one boat with six men commanded by Josiah Smith, a private. They afterwards proceeded to New London and burnt the town. We were received by the garrison with enthusiasm, being considered experienced artillerists, whom they much needed, and we were immediately assigned to our stations. The fort was an oblong square, with bastions at opposite angles, its longest side fronting the river in a north-west and south-east direction. Its walls were of stone, and were ten or twelve feet high on the lower side, and surrounded by a ditch. On the wall were pickets, projecting over twelve feet; above this was a parapet with embrasures, and within a platform for the cannon, and a step to mount upon to shoot over the parapet with small arms. In the south-west bastion was a flag-staff, and in the side, near the opposite angle, was the gate, in front of which was a triangular breast-work to protect the gate; and to the right of this was a redoubt, with a three-pounder in it, which was about 120 yards from the gate. Between the fort and the river was another battery, with a covered way, but which could not be used in this attack, as the enemy appeared in a different quarter. The garrison, with the volunteers, consisted of about 160 men. Soon after our arrival the enemy appeared in force in some woods about half a mile southeast of the fort, from whence they sent a flag of truce, which was met by Captain Shapley, demanding an unconditional surrender, threatening at the same time, to storm the fort instantly if the terms were not accepted.[1] A council of war was held, and it was the unanimous voice, that the garrison were unable to defend themselves against so superior a force. But a militia colonel who was then in the fort, and had a body of men in the immediate vicinity, said he would reinforce them with 2 or 300 men in fifteen minutes, if they would hold out; Colonel Ledyard agreed to send back a defiance, upon the most solemn assurance of immediate succour. For this purpose Colonel ——— started, his men being then in sight; but he was no more seen, nor did he even attempt

---

[1] Lieutenant-Colonel Eyre formed his men behind the ledge of rocks which forms the eastern boundary of the burial-ground. Major Montgomery's column formed in the rear of a hillock, a short distance northeast of that point.

a diversion in our favor.   When the answer to their demand
had been returned by Captain Shapley, the enemy were
soon in motion, and marched with great rapidity, in a solid
column, to within a short distance of the fort, where divid-
ing the column, they rushed furiously and simultaneously
to the assault of the southwest bastion and the opposite
sides.   They were, however, repulsed with great slaughter,
their commander mortally wounded, and Major Montgomery, next in rank, killed, having been thrust through the
body, whilst in the act of scaling the walls at the south-west
bastion, by Captain Shapley.   The command then devolved
on Colonel Beckwith, a refugee from New Jersey, who
commanded a corps of that description.   The enemy rallied
and returned the attack with great vigor, but were received
and repulsed with equal firmness.   During the attack a
shot cut the halyards of the flag, and it fell to the ground,
but was instantly remounted on a pike pole.   This accident
proved fatal to us, as the enemy, supposed it had been
struck by its defenders, rallied again, and rushing with re-
doubled impetuosity, carried the south-west bastion by
storm.   Until this moment our loss was trifling in number,
being six or seven killed, and eighteen or twenty wounded.
Never was a post more bravely defended, nor a garrison
more barbarously butchered.   We fought with all kinds of
weapons, and at all places, with a courage that deserved a
better fate.[1]   Many of the enemy were killed under the

---

[1] John Daboll, one of the garrison, discharged his musket no less than
seven times at one particular soldier, who also seems to have singled him
out as his opponent.   The singular duel was terminated by the eighth
shot from the enemy carrying away the lock of Daboll's musket, and severely wounding him in the head.   This incident was related to the
writer by an old gentleman now living in Groton, who had frequently
heard the story from Daboll.—H.

Thomas, son of Lieutenant Parke Avery, aged seventeen, was killed
fighting by the side of his father.   Just before he fell (the battle growing

walls by throwing simple shot over on them, and never would we have relinquished our arms, had we had the least idea that such a catastrophe would have followed. To describe this scene I must be permitted to go back a little in my narrative. I commanded an eighteen-pounder on the south side of the gate, and while in the act of fighting my gun, a ball passed through the embrasure, struck me a little above the right ear, grazing the skull, and cutting off the veins, which bled profusely. A handkerchief was tied around it, and I continued at my duty. Discovering, some little time after, that a British soldier had broken a picket at the bastion on my left, and was forcing himself through the hole, whilst the men stationed there were gazing at the battle which raged opposite to them, cried, "my brave fellows the enemy are breaking in behind you," and raised my pike to dispatch the intruder, when a ball struck my left arm at the elbow, and my pike fell to the ground. Nevertheless I grasped it with my right hand, and with the men, who turned and fought manfully, cleared the breach. The enemy, however, soon after forced the south-west bastion, where Captain Shapley, Captain Peter Richards, Lieutenant Richard Chapman, and several other men of distinction, and volunteers, had fought with unconquerable courage, and were all either killed or mortally wounded, and which had sustained the brunt of every attack.

Captain P. Richards, Lieutenant Chapman, and several others, were killed in the bastion; Captain Shapley and others wounded. He died of his wounds in January following.

Colonel Ledyard, seeing the enemy within the fort, gave

---

hot) the father turned and said, "Tom, my son, do your duty!" "Never fear, father," was the reply, and the next moment he was stretched upon the ground. "'Tis a good cause," said the father, and he remained firm at his post.—*Caulkins.*

orders to cease firing, and to throw down our arms, as the fort had surrendered.   We did so, but they continued firing upon us, crossed the fort and opened the gate, when they marched in, firing in platoons upon those who were retreating to the magazine and barrack-rooms for safety.   At this moment the renegade Colonel Beckwith commanding, cried out, "Who commands this garrison?"   Colonel Ledyard, who was standing near me, answered, "I did sir, but you do now," at the same time stepping forward, handed him his sword with the point towards himself.   At this instant I perceived a soldier in the act of bayoneting me from behind.   I turned suddenly round and grasped his bayonet, endeavoring to unship it, and knock off the thrust, but in vain.   Having but one hand, he succeeded in forcing it into my right hip, above the joint, and just below the abdomen, and crushed me to the ground.   The first person I saw afterwards was my brave commander, a corpse by my side, having been run through the body with his own sword, by the savage renegade.   Never was a scene of more brutal wanton carnage witnessed than now took place. The enemy were still firing upon us in platoons, and in the barrack-rooms, which were continued for some minutes, when they discovered they were in danger of being blown up, by communicating fire to the powder scattered at the mouth of the magazine while delivering out cartridges; nor did it then cease in the rooms for some minutes longer. All this time the bayonet was "freely used," even on those who were helplessly wounded and in the agonies of death. I recollect Captain William Seymour,[1] a volunteer from Hartford, had thirteen bayonet wounds, although his knee had previously been shattered by a ball, so much so, that it was obliged to be amputated the next day.   But I need not mention particular cases.   I have already said that we

---

[1] Nephew of Colonel Ledyard.

had six killed and eighteen wounded previous to their storming our lines; eighty-five were killed in all, thirty-five mortally and dangerously wounded, and forty taken prisoners to New York, most of them slightly hurt.

After the massacre they plundered us of every thing we had, and left us literally naked. When they commenced gathering us up together with their own wounded, they put theirs under the shade of the platform, and exposed us to the sun, in front of the barracks, where we remained over an hour. Those that could stand were then paraded, and ordered to the landing, while those that could not (of which number I was one) were put in one of our ammunition wagons, and taken to the brow of the hill, (which was very steep, and at least one hundred rods in descent,) from whence it was permitted to run down by itself, but was arrested in its course, near the river, by an apple tree. The pain and anguish we all endured in this rapid descent, as the wagon jumped and jostled over rocks and holes is inconceivable; and the jar in its arrest was like bursting the cords of life asunder, and caused us to shriek with almost supernatural force. Our cries were distinctly heard and noticed on the opposite side of the river, (which is a mile wide,) amidst all the confusion which raged in burning and sacking the town. We remained in the wagon more than an hour before our humane conquerors hunted us up, when we were again paraded and laid on the beach, preparatory to embarkation; but by the interposition of Ebenezer Ledyard, brother to Colonel Ledyard, who humanely represented our deplorable situation, and the impossibility of our being able to reach New York, thirty-five of us were paroled in the usual form. Being near the house of Ebenezer Avery, who was also one of our number, we were taken into it. Here we had not long remained before a marauding party set fire to every room, evidently intending to burn us up with the house. The party soon left it, when it was with difficulty extinguished, and we were thus saved from the flames.[1] Ebenezer Ledyard again interfered, and obtained a sentinel to remain and guard us until the last of the enemy embarked—about 11 o'clock at night. None of our own people came to us till near daylight the next morning, not knowing previous to that time that the enemy had departed.

Such a night of distress and anguish was scarcely ever passed by mortal. Thirty-five of us were lying on the bare floor, stiff, mangled, and wounded in every manner, exhausted with pain, fatigue, and loss of blood, without clothes or any thing to cover us, trembling with cold and spasms of extreme anguish, without fire or light, parched with excruciating thirst, not a wound dressed, nor a soul to administer to one of our wants, nor an assisting hand to turn us during these long tedious hours of the night. Nothing but groans and unavailing sighs were heard, and two of our number did not live to see the light of the morning, which brought with it some ministering angels to our relief. The first was in the person of Miss Fanny Ledyard, of Southold, L. I., then on a visit to her uncle, our murdered commander, who held to my lips a cup of warm chocolate, and soon after returned with wine and other refreshments, which revived us a little. For these kindnesses she has never ceased to receive my most grateful thanks, and fervent prayers for her felicity.

The cruelty of our enemy can not be conceived, and our renegade countrymen surpassed in this respect, if possible, our British foes. We were at least an hour after the battle within a few steps of a pump in the garrison, well supplied with water, and, although we were suffering with

---

[1] This is the second house on the right side of the main street, south of the ferry; it is now occupied by Simon Huntington, Esq.

thirst, they would not permit us to take one drop of it, nor give us any themselves. Some of our number, who were not disabled from going to the pump, were repulsed with the bayonet; and not one drop did I taste after the action commenced, although begging for it after I was wounded of all who came near me, until relieved by Miss Ledyard. We were a horrible sight at this time. Our own friends did not know us—even my own wife came in the room in search of me, and did not recognize me, and as I did not see her, she left the room to seek for me among the slain, who had been collected under a large elm tree near the house. It was with the utmost difficulty that many of them could be identified, and we were frequently called upon to assist their friends in distinguishing them, by remembering particular wounds, &c. Being myself taken out by two men for this purpose, I met my wife and brother, who, after my wounds were dressed by Dr. Downer, from Preston, took me—not to my own home, for that was in ashes, as also every article of my property, furniture, and clothing—but to my brother's, where I lay eleven months as helpless as a child, and to this day feel the effects of it severely.

Such was the battle of Groton Heights; and such, as far as my imperfect manner and language can describe, a part of the sufferings which we endured. Never, for a moment, have I regretted the share I had in it. I would, for an equal degree of honor, and the prosperity which has resulted to my country from the Revolution, be willing, if possible, to suffer it again.

STEPHEN HEMPSTEAD.

6

NARRATIVE

OF

JOHN HEMPSTEAD.

I NOW Setdown to give a narrative of My proseding on the 6th Day of Sept., 1781. All tho itt is forty-eight years Sense the town of New London was Sack'd and Burnt By the British Solders under the command of that infamas trater Benedick Arnel, itt is formillyer as iff it was transacted yesterday. In the morning of the sd day I was att my house in bed between Brake of Day and Sunrise. I hard the Signel of arlarm by the fireing of thre Cannon, althow Our Signol was two cannon near to gether; they fir'd 3 to Deceve; however I turn'd Out and ask'd my wife to git Brakefast as soon as possabel for I must go off. I went Down on the hill about half mild Distant, now caled prospect hill, Whare the fleet was in fare Site in a line acrost the haber. There was 15 Sale of Ships an other Square rig'd Vesels, besides other Vesels. I came home. My brakefast was redy. After Brakefast I Said to my Son John to take the team & go intown and Bring out his granmother Bill. My hors Being redy I Slung my Musket & Cartrig Box and mounted with my littel Black Boy to bring the hors Back. Expeting to find people att the alarum post at Manwaring hill. After I got Under Way my wife Called to me pretty loud. I Stopt my hors and ask'd her What She wanted. Her answer was Not to let me hear that you are Shot in the Back.

1 proseded to the alarum post and found nobody thare. I rode down into the Strete, where my father formerly liv'd, and gave up my hors to my black Boy, and Started on a foot, which was on my way to my Lit Collon harris, but was overtaken by Capt. John Deshon and Capt. Mickel Malley. They asked mee to gitt up Behind One of thim & I Did, but I hav forgot which. We Sune got to Col. Haris, & I Saw him Standing on his Dore Stone. I Slipt of the hors & met the Colo half the way from his house to the highway with a Short willow Stick in his hand. My reply to him was what is the news Colo? he replid the Enemy are landing att Brown's farm. What is the order? his answer go Down & make the best Defence you Can with what men you Can gitt. I hope you will go with me. his answer I have Been Sencherd for not giving timely notis. You had Beter go with mee & So wee parted. I went Down to Brown's farm. I got there Sometime Before they landed & there was But about forty men arm'd. Wee watted while the enemy was maning there botes. After they ware all mand they Opend there bride Sides upon Both Shores, and all landed under ther Cannon whos balls flew over Our heads like hale Stones untill they ware all landed. itt was verry Still. there was One man Drest in Red Stud up in the Starn of One of the botes, with his Sword Drawn & Brandishing itt Over his head, & Said Pull a way, God Dam you, Pull away, which I thaught wass arnald. the men Sune landed and form'd a line from Lester' gut to the White Beach & the Enemy adVansed with a Slow march untill they got upon high Ground, & then they went quick from one wall to another, and wee Retreted Exchangen Shot every Opertunty. We Continued untill wee Brought them within Cannon Shot of the fort On town hill, Vulgarly Called fort Nonsense. When the forte opened upon the Enemy the Shot fell Short, &

wee ware between two fires. Capt. Wm. Coit Spoke to
me as he had no Commanding posision for God Sake Send
or go to the fort to Stop the fireing.   I told him to go him
Self. he Repld that he had no Command.   I told him
then go in my name, & he Went, & the fireing Seased.
We Retreted, and Sune got near the fort att the house of
Wm. Hempsted.   he Called to mee and asked me iff I
wolde take Sum jinn.   I told him yes & thanky two.   I
went to his dore next the Street, & he had a Case of hol-
land jinn, which was well Excepted.   Wm. was harnest
redy to march.   as itt hapen'd Capt. Willam Coit, Capt.
Richard Deshon, Capt. Jonathan Calkins, & Capt. Nathll
Salstanstell, which I Hed not Sean before that day.   We
all Drank & Desperst, Wm. Hempsted and all.   I spoke
to Sd Hempsted if he was going to leave his Case of jin
there; he Said itt was no matter whare it was, the Dogs
will find itt.   Come take hold of One handil, and wee
Carred itt west of his house, about Six rod, to a pease of
patoes with high weads, & wee bent the weades over
them & they never fownd the case of jin.   And then wee
Despers'd.   While wee ware there I presev'd that the Enemy fil'd of from the left, as thoe there Intention was to
Soround the fort.   by this time there wass more peopel got
there, & I spoke to them.   Who will goe along with mee?
Mr. George Smith sd I will go.   With that two more Said
I will go with you, & wee went to the northwest over the
hill, and we posted Our Selves In a Very advatagos place.
We Soon Saw thee enemy Comming; wee Saw ther bag-
nert above the corn advancing in a Ingan file.   We before
the Enemy made any Stand we a gread to Reserve our fire.
they Said One and all lit Us fire.   I told them I would reserve my fire and wate for Orders.   Very Will, the Enemy
by this time had got up to a Stone wall about Six rods in
Our frunt.   this Wall was on Our lefhand.   When they

ware 12 or 15 in number I gave the word fire. it was no
Suner Sad then Dun. the Enemy return'd the fire, but the
men went to the foart as I supos'd. By this time perhaps
25 men had Got in a huddel. I arose took Good ame. I
Sea that they ware Confused. I took a cartrig out of my
Box. But they Sune return'd the fire. But Before I could
Load my pease two men with grene Cotes and long fethers
gumt over the wall with ther peases upon Recover. J Re-
membr what I thought. I can git as fur from the Wall
as they ware. I run towarde the fort. that was about 30
Rod Distant. I had got but about Six Rod from the wall.
I look'd Over my Sholder when their Guns flasht, but hapy
for mee one of thir balls Struck a potato hill, clos by my
feet, and the other whistled by my hed. I Rember what
I thaught that they ware not Very good marks men.

I Repar'd to the fort and found nobody there. I found
a quille[1] of Riging on the prade. I Rold itt under the
platform & went Out of the Gates, & turned to the right
into the Intrenchment, & as I was in the intrenchment the
Enemy fired upon Mee & ther Shot scoward the Dich On
both Sides of Mee. I got Round the corner & was Sum
putoit[2] to get up the dich however I got up & over in
Esq. Millers Orchard, which was Very thick and ful of
leaves. By this time the Enemy got into the fort & husard,
and they were answerd By a man, "Wilkom God damyou
to fort Non Sence." I look'd and Saw the man behind a
tree. I got behind another & they gave us a shot in the
orchard, but to no purpus. I mad the beste of my way
touards town. I got near David holtes, Now John Coites,
I heard Cannon On manworng hill. I made my way to
the sd hill cross lots there. I found 2 feald peases, & Near
a hundred men Olmost unarm'd. there I found Capt. Richard Deshon & Wm. Ashcraft, which Stuck By the Stuff,

---

[1] Coil of rigging.   [2] Put to it.

when as the Enemy advanced they all left us, But wee gave
them two Shot.   as the Enemy apeard in Sight the peaple
all fled except Capt. Deshon & Wm. Ashcraft.   I told
Capt. Deshon we would not be kild with Our One wepens.
I Sholderd a Sack of Cartridg's & Deshon the Ramer &
Spunge Ladel, and put them under the Brig By Chapman
house, & I put the Cartridges In Robart Manworings lott
and Bent the tops of weds over them.   I niver Sau Deshon
after that for the day.   After I hid the Cartrgs I went down
the hill.   I intended to git Behind Rich'd Chapmons Barn.
I Rec'd a Volly of Shot I Judg'd about 20.   the Shot Cut
thrugh the grass on Both Sid of me.   I must Riturn back
to manworing hill.   before Wee left the hill I Spok to Wm.
ashcraft to go to Chapmans house & get Sunthing to Spike
up the Guns, & I Spoke Sumthing Starn to him, & he Stopt
& said there will bee nobody har when I Com Back.   yes
I will be hear.   hee went.   my speaking Loud Sumbody
Cald to me and Said, what Do you want, & I look'd & itt
wass Coln. Haris, whith I never see Sense morning with the
same Stick.   harris went into the house & brought Out the
Shank of a Spike Gimblet, which answered no purpos.   I
riturn'd Behind Chapmans Barn.   I went from the Barn
toward the highway to a pare of Bars, & as I was Giting
over the Bars, a musket Bal stuck into the lim of a apel
tree that Brancht over the bars about two feet from my
head.   then I made my way for home for this Reason.
my father Died Lately, & his estate not Setled,[1] I had all

---

[1] In the Gazette of September 7th, the day following the battle, is the
following notice:

   " All persons that are indebted to the estate of JOHN HEMPSTED,
Esq., late of *New London*, decesd, by book or note, are once more called
upon in the most pressing manner to settle the same, or they must not
take it amiss if after this notice they should be called upon in a more
disagreeable manner, which they may spedily expect (without respect of
persons) should they neglect a compliance with this request.
                                        JOHN HEMPSTED, *Executor.*
New London, Sept. 4th, 1781.   6—w

his Books & papers att my house. But I Coold not Git hom no other way but to go round mr. Winthrops house, By being Sorround by the enemy. I had not got more then half the way to where magor Richards after liv'd I Saw the Enemy on the top of mr. Winthrups house. I maid my way to qaker hill, & there I found I Should say 5 hunderd men, sum arm'd & sum no armes. while I was there majer Darrow Come Riding Down, & Said to the men why the Devel dont yoo Go down & meet the Ene- my? Picket Latimer sd as he was there that he would not Resk his life to Save other mens property, tho he was the Capt. of the Endependt Cumpany att that time. (Lat- imer was Burnt first.) I then mad the best of my Way hom & packt up my fathers papers & books & Carid them into the Swamp taking my Sun John & young James Smith With mee that they might find them if I didnot Come Back. I Eat my Dinner & Sett out agane to follow the Enemy, but passing Daniel Latimers, whare I supose thare was a hundred men, I past them and had gott 20 or 30 Rods By, Colo. Latimer Cauld to me to Cum back. I Re- pl'd I could not, I was In persute of the enemy. his Re- ply to me was, I Command You to com back. then I Stopt & Went back. he Detaned mee abot one½ anower, & Sent with me 2 other men, but whilst I was thare Capt. John mcCarty & David Robart Came Riding up to the Doare and Said Whare is that Dam'd tory, & they Rusht in to the house, & I Clost to there heels, they saing whare is that Damid Tory. they was stopt with the point of the baganet, by a Solder that stud as a gard Over Thos. Fitch, whih ware taken near Black point with a Drove of Sheep to Send to the Enemy. I Return. On my progres from Latimers I Shapt my Cours a cross lots. in Crossing Sam- uel Garners lot about forty or fifty Rod West of Robart Manworings house, I Come a Crost a man that was Shot

Throug the body with a musket ball. I had sum Descorse with him & found out who hee was. I found him to be What was Cauled & Refege. I left him & past on. before I got halv way from Where John Coits now lives & Col. Harris, I mett sum men Brengin Sam'el B. Hempsted in a blanket. he had a Shot throug his thi. I wint a littel further & I met Sum more men Brengin Jonathan whaly whih was wounde. the Enemy had Gott So far & so few to follow, I Riturnd back into the town, which was then all in ashes. I got to Mr. Shaws Stone house whih was on fire on the Ruf. this must Sarve for this Day, excepting I Returnd home & found nearly one hundred peple woming & Children. The next Day I wint to groten, & when I got over the other Side there I saw Liet. Richard Chapman, John Holt, & John Cleark, in a Bote Dead to bee Cared to New London. I went to the fort on Groten hill to See the Carnag which was Dredfull to Behold. there was about twenty men lay Dead Side by Side. we found one man under the platfm Dead, & there ware a Great many of the enemy In the Ditch Round the Redout, which is before the Gate, how many I Cant tell, for they ware not taken out Whilst I was there. But the Enemy Intended to blow up the fort for they Stroed a train of powder from the gate to the magesean & itt burnt from the gate about half way to the magesean, and the Comunication was cut of by a mans fingers which lay in the durt. I Stay'd there until all most night & I went home. the 3 Day I took my hors and Went to town hill, to fourt Nonsence, as itt Was Call'd, & as I was Seting on my

hors looking into the fort, Mr. William Hempstead Called to mee. I asked him Watt he Wanted. his answer wass Cum & Drink Sum of Your Jin, & I wint to him. he Sase to me I have Got the Jin. the Dogs hav not found itt. through your means I Saved it. He said to me which way did you go when you left me. I told him that I was Jellos that the enemy was Going to Surround us & cut us of from the fort. I Saw them filing of from there left Wing, as tho that was thar Desine. I went over into Mr. Ways lot. I Saw them advans. I saw ther Byonets over the Growing Corn, & wee three in number lay In ambush in a very safe place, & the Enemy advancin in an Indian file, they advansed to a Stone Wall that Coverd our left hand. Wee lay conseald untill they Gethered; about a Dusen or fifteen had Colected. I Bid them to fire. I had agred before that I would Reserve my fire. they Ware about Six rod Distant from us. they Deschargd there peases & run to the fort. they returnd the fire by this time. I supose about twenty Colected. then I arose & Gave them a Shot & Run toward the fort. Hempsted, he sade, Did you Know you kild any of them. I Didnot carting.[1] well there Was two Kild, and wee went to See & It was as Evident as that there had been two hogs kild, By the blood & whare they Draged them away through a feald of potoes, & ther Sholders tore up the potatoes out of the hills.

From the three Black marks on the other Side Back of this Was the Descorse that past Between Wm. Hempsted and myself on the 3d Day after. I had the command of a company of militia of forty men, & I never Saw but Seven of them that day, as they lived upon the Shore, and ther famely ware exposed to the ravagis of the Enemy.

The Fore going is What I past throug the 6th Day of Septr., 1781.

JOHN HEMPSTED.

---

[1] Certain.

7

THE EXPERIENCE

OF

JONATHAN BROOKS,

AT NEW LONDON ON THE 6TH OF SEPTEMBER, 1781.

MY father, who belonged to what was called the In-
dependent Company in the militia, and was also a
business man, rose at early dawn and walked down to the
bank so called, which was the lookout for the harbor.
There he saw the enemy's fleet at the mouth of the harbor,
and quickly returned and took me down with him to see
what was going on. The fleet had not then all anchored,
but were dropping in by the western point fast. He said,
"they are going to land; go home, take the bridle and get
the horse from the pasture as quickly as possible." I did
so, and the horse was soon at the door, the pasture being
about a mile and a half off. The horse was then loaded
with a bed and some clothing and other valuables. My
father then mounted and was gone about one hour and a
half, and on returning said he had deposited his load and
provided quarters for his family at a place he named, about
two miles and a half distant. He then gave directions that
my brothers Nathan, seven, and John, five years of age,
should drive the cow to the rendezvous and remain there,
and that my mother and sister should repair thither with all
possible speed.

He then armed and equipped himself, mounted his horse,

taking me behind him to bring the horse back, telling the family I should be left in charge of the house when I returned. There I was to await the arrival of the enemy in case they succeeded in carrying the fort and town, at the same time charging me to treat them civilly, and furnish them with whatever they called for that the house afforded —which at that time was well stocked with good things; that he himself should, in case he was not killed or badly wounded, and the enemy made good their landing and could not be defeated or stopped, retreat back to his property, which was in buildings and his all, and there make a stand and act according to circumstances. We rode by the fort gate on the lower road, meaning to go to the lighthouse by White Beach, but on coming to the beach it was found that the enemy's small craft were so near in that we could see the soldiers plainly, and hear them converse. The ships at this time kept up a heavy cannonade; we then left the shore and struck for the heights across the lots. Being unacquainted we came to a place that was miry, and very difficult for the horse to pass through; in short he stuck fast, and we then dismounted and got the horse out of the mire. Before we re-mounted, being but a little distance from where the horse mired, a shot passed through the thicket directly across where we stood to disentangle him, and cut off several saplings of the size of a man's wrist. Whether we were discovered by the ships and fired at or whether it was a chance shot I know not; at any rate it made us look around. We then made for the cross road that connects the upper and lower roads. At the head of the road we fell in with about one hundred citizens, volunteer soldiers armed and equipped. My father dismounted and joined them. The party then fell into conversation about how they should manage, having no commanding officer. Some who had no experience in war matters were for fighting at any odds, saying, "let us form where we are and contest the ground inch by inch;" but Captain Nathaniel Saltonstall, who once commanded the ship Putnam, said, "gentlemen, whether I have as much courage as many who have given their opinion, I shall not undertake to say; but this I will say, for one I will not be such a fool as to stand here open breasted and be shot down by the very first volley of the enemy's fire." The enemy were at this time in sight marching in solid columns. At this juncture Colonel Harris rode up with his sword by his side. I can this instant—in imagination—see him. The band were all much elated at seeing him, saying, "now, colonel, we have somebody to command us, and are at your service." The colonel replied, "You must excuse me, gentlemen, as I have a violent sick-headache this morning, and can hardly sit on my horse," then turning his horse and riding off. This conduct of the colonel so enraged many of the people that they were almost like madmen, some cocking and presenting their guns, which were loaded, exclaiming, "let's shoot the d—d rascal." The party now left to themselves, on the sober second thought hapened to hit upon Captain Saltonstall, to whom they now looked to command them, and asked him what they should do—there was no time for parley now. He said, "My advice is to divide ourselves into two parties, each taking the stone wall which is on each side of the road for our shelter; each man take care of himself, and get a shot at the enemy as best he can." This course was taken, and Benedict Arnold and his army of traitors (for they were almost all of them refugees) were much annoyed by them. My father now told me to return home, put the horse in the barn, and await the arrival of himself or the enemy. I mounted and rode as far as Fort Nonsense, on Town Hill. Seeing quite a bustle there, and having some notion of seeing the fight, I hitched my horse to the wall, and mounted to the top of a very tall sycamore tree. I stayed in the top of the tree until I saw the drag-ropes fixed to the field-pieces and manned for retreat. I then took myself down not very slow, and was off. Directly afterd I fell in with a great booby of a boy whom I knew; he was crying; he said his horse had thrown him, and he wished to go to his Uncle Harris's, the colonel's, almost opposite Fort Nonsense.¹ I said to him, Charles, if you go that way you may see trouble. He cried, and I assisted him to re-mount, and my horse soon cut dirt for for home. I was inquired of as I passed, and I told them the enemy had landed, and would be upon them in a twink-ling. There was motion and commotion then in good earn-est. I arrived safe home, put the horse in the barn accord-ing to orders, and then seated myself in a conspicuous place on the side of the street, waiting with anxiety to see the red coats enter Bradley Street. All was perfect silence, and there seemed to be a kind of solemnity reigning in the place.² The silence was soon broken by the entrance of five or six shabby looking fellows into the street on the full run from the south. They passed me without notice, so in-tent were they probably on the prospect before them, for they shouted as they passed, "by G–d, we'll have fine plun-der by-and-by." Very soon I heard a great noise, and I mounted higher on the fence and looked in the direction that the noise proceeded from and saw the doors of a store-house³ open, which contained the goods of the prize ship

---

¹ The house occupied at that time by Colonel Harris is still preserved, and known to the citizens of New London as the "Robinson House," now owned by Thomas Fitch, Esq.

² Bradley Street, at that time containing twelve to fifteen buildings, consisting mostly of humble dwellings, entirely escaped the conflagration.

³ This store-house was situated on "the beach," (Water Street,) the second street below that in which Brooks had taken his stand of observa-tion.

Hannah, the invoice of which was £80,000 sterling. The goods were flying out of the store, and I should think thirty or forty persons were loading themselves with plunder and scampering off.

I now heard the call of my mother, who I supposed had gone and left the house. She inquired where the horse was, and on being informed told me to get it and bring it to the door as quick as possible. I did so. She then brought a large sack, saying, "these are very valuable papers of your father's,[1] and you must take them out to your Uncle Richard's," (the place provided for the family to flee to.) I remonstrated, saying, "my father's orders were not to leave the house, and that I should lose the chance of seeing the Regulars"—for so the British troops were then called. But she urged me to go, saying, "go, my son, you can get back time enough to see them; I shall follow directly after you." I did go, but I had not proceeded fifty rods before I heard the musketry going crack, crack, on the whole westerly side of the town. I, however, moved quickly on, and when I came to the head of the cove the street was so crowded with the fleeing women and children, all loaded with something, that I had to move slowly. They inquired where the enemy were. I said, "they will be among you within five minutes if you delay." Their loading was soon thrown down, and they started on a quick pace.[2] I passed on, turning the corner toward Post Hill,

---

[1] Lieutenant Richard Chapman, who fell that day in the defense of Fort Griswold.

[2] Miss Caulkins, in writing of the terrible consternation and alarm of this day, relates the following affecting incident:

"Amid the bustle of these scenes, when each one was laden with what was nearest at hand or dearest to his heart, one man was seen hastening alone to the burial-ground, with a small coffin under his arm. His child had died the day before, and he could not leave it unburied. In haste and trepidation he threw up the mold, and deposited his precious burden; then covering it quickly and setting up a stone to mark the place, he hurried away to secure other beloved ones from a more cruel spoiler."

and when I turned the corner into the Cohanzy Road the bullets flew whistling over my head at no small rate; I just went clear and that was all, for the enemy were in possession of Post Hill. I went with my bag of papers to the place directed, and went out and gathered peaches, for to return to town at this time was out of the question. In about one hour my mother arrived. She inquired of me where Nathan and John were. It will be recollected that they were sent with the cow in the morning. I told her I had not seen them. She appeared to be violently agitated and alarmed, and at length she said: "Get up the horse and look for them; go here, go there, go every where"—all in a breath. I did go, and rode and rode, and returned and reported no tidings of the boys, and off again, until at length I was almost wrought up into a frenzy myself. I then made up my mind to cross over to Quaker Hill, on the Norwich road, and if I could not hear of them there, to enter the town at all hazards, for I conceived it possible that being unable to drive the cow where directed, for she was in her former pasture, that they were disheartened, and had returned to the house in town, and as the town was on fire, might, as I conceived, be burnt in the house. My God, how my heart-strings vibrated at this idea! Go ahead and save them, says I. With much difficulty I crossed over the lots —an unknown way to me—to the Norwich road, and made fruitless inquiries.

The militia from Norwich and the adjacent country had arrived, commanded by a Colonel Rogers, I believe, and were ordered to halt on the hill. I, however, pushed on for the town, but was immediately stopped by a sentinel, who inquired where I was going. I replied, "into New London." He said, "you can not go, the enemy are there." I told him I must and should go, come what might. The soldier, seeing my determination, seized my bridle and lifted me off the horse and sent me to the colonel. The colonel told me that he was very busy, but that I must not go into town. He was then conversing with his officers about going on a reconnoitering party to a projecting point of land that hung, as it were, over the town. As soon as the party were mounted I stepped up to the colonel and said, "Sir, will you please to let me go with you?" He replied, "certainly, my lad." I mounted my horse and followed along in the rear. When we came to the brink of the hill the party turned to the left into a private road that led to a farm, in order to gain the point of observation. At this time they were much engaged in conversation. Now's your time, says I to myself; go it, Jenny—for that was the name of the mare—and I put on the string. I entered the north end of the town, passed into Main Street about twenty rods. when the heat and smoke of the burning buildings was such that I could not urge the mare on. I, however, retreated back about twenty rods, put on the whip, and she went through. I had just cleared the burning district at that point, when there was a store, containing a large quantity of gunpowder, blew up, which filled the air with smoke and fragments, which fell around me in every direction. I, however, jogged on unharmed, passed into Bradley Street, where my father's principal buildings were, none of which were burnt, and I satisfied myself that there was no one in the house we occupied. I saw a heavy fire raging on the parade, which was the Court House, Jail, Episcopal Church, &c. I, of course, could not pass that way, and, indeed, the smoke was so dense—there being but little wind—no object whatever could be discovered. I retraced my steps, passed again into Main Street, turned the corner to the right into State Street. No object at this point was discernable on the parade, owing to the density of the smoke. I rode on till opposite the printing office of Timothy Green, Esq., where in the street flat on his back lay a drunken British soldier with his gun bayoneted lying beside him. This, I thought, was a good prize, so I slipped softly off of the horse and seized the gun. His cartridge-box and bayonet-sheath were slung to him, and I did not attempt to meddle with them for fear of waking him. I made several attempts in various ways to mount with the gun, but could not succeed, and so I threw it over the fence and left him, thinking I would let well enough alone.

I now passed out of town to Rockdale Place, where my Grandfather Chapman lived, and still no news of my brothers.

After leaving Rockdale I fell in with Colonel Latimer and a flock of old tories, whose names I could mention if so disposed. To Colonel Latimer I told the place and situation of the British soldier, which he said he would have attended to. The soldier was found and detained a prisoner—not. however, by the colonel's means. I was disappointed in not finding my father at the house as he had appointed, and concluded that he was either killed, wounded, or a prisoner; but he was neither. At the time I was in the house he, with a few more inhabitants that were in town, were engaged in the smoke on the parade trying to arrest the progress of the fire, and stop it from passing into Bradley Street, which they succeeded in doing, and saved that part of the town.

Thus you may understand that I passed through the principal streets of New London on the afternoon of the 6th of September, 1781, and never saw a single living creature, except one singed cat, that ran across the street when the store blew up; the soldier was not living, certainly, for he was dead drunk.   I was the first person that entered the town after the retreat of the enemy, and from circumstances must have been directly at their heels.   My uncle, Richard Chapman, lieutenant under Captain Adam Shaply, at Fort Trumbull, was killed in the massacre at Fort Griswold, on the heights opposite New London, on that disastrous day.

JONATHAN BROOKS,

Post Hill, 1840.

A NARRATIVE

OF THE

Battle on Groton Heights,

SEPTEMBER 6TH, 1781,

BY

AVERY DOWNER, M. D.,

ASSISTANT SURGEON OF THE EIGHTH REGIMENT OF
CONNECTICUT MILITIA.

ON the morning of the 6th of September, 1781, a British fleet of twenty-four sail was discovered entering the harbor of New London. Arnold, the commander, being a native of Norwich, and well acquainted with the river and harbor, which was of much service to him, and also many tories and traitors of equal infamy with himself accompanied him, which is evidence that traitors indulge more revenge than a common enemy.

I performed militia military duty as rank and file, by detachment from my company and regiment at Fort Griswold, a number of times during the summer of 1779. In 1781 I served as an assistant surgeon of the 8th regiment of Connecticut militia, including Fort Griswold in its limits I well remember the morning of the alarm two guns from the fort in a given time was the alarm. This the enemy well understood, and they fired a third, by which we in Preston were deceived, being fourteen miles distant. Doctor Joshua Downer, my father, and surgeon of the said 8th regiment, said to me and others in the morning that the firing must be an alarm; but it was doubted, until the smoke of New London appeared like a cloud, which I well remember. My father immediately started for the fort and ordered me to follow him.

On his arrival near the meeting-house he met Benjamin Bill and others who had escaped from the enemy slightly wounded. He dressed their wounds, and proceeded to the house of James Bailey, where he found Charles Eldridge wounded in the knee. He dressed him and proceeded, by orders from the field officers of his regiment, to the house of Ebenezer Avery. The surviving British commander, Bloomfield, had ordered all the wounded to be collected on the bank of the river near the house. All that were able to go to New York were sent down to the shipping; the remainder were paroled and left.

Soon after the enemy were gone my father and Doctor Prentiss went into the house and took charge of forty wounded men. I got to their assistance at about twelve o'clk at night. Captain Youngs Ledyard and one more died before morning. By daylight all were taken care of, and we with others went into the fort. When we came to Colonel Ledyard, the friend and neighbor of Doctor Prentiss, he exclaimed, "Oh my God, I can not endure this!"

Our dead were by the enemy mostly left on the parade in front of the barracks; their dead they buried in the ditch, of a triangular work, made to cover the gate. Major Montgomery they buried on the right of the gate as we pass out, which I well remember. According to Arnold's dispatches to His Excellency Sir Henry Clinton, dated Plum Island, September 8th, 1781, it appears that the forces which he sent on the Groton side of the river consisted of the 40th and 54th British regiments, and the 3d battalion of New Jersey volunteers, with a detachment of Yaggers and artillery, all under the command of Lieutenant-Colonel Eyre.

Arnold landed his division on the New London side of the river, and was informed by friends that Fort Griswold contained only about twenty or thirty men. In this his good friends deceived him, for in his dispatches he says that the defence was so obstinate that he sent an officer to countermand his order for assault just as the fort was carried. Fort Trumbull on the New London side of the river was little more than a water battery open from behind, and the enemy coming in that direction the men spiked their guns and crossed the river and went into Fort Griswold.

On the approach of the British the commander sent a Captain Beckwith, a Jersey refugee, to demand a surrender of the fort. Colonel Ledyard ordered a shot fired in front, which stopped the flag. He then sent Captain Amos Stanton and Captain Shapley with his flag; the demand of Beckwith was refused and the flags returned.

Eyre and Montgomery then advanced their columns, and the attack commenced on three sides of the fort at the same time.

In about forty minutes the assailants entered the fort. According to Arnold's dispatches, before referred to, as published in Green's paper of New London, (*Connecticut Gazette,*) it appears that his loss was—

KILLED.	WOUNDED.
1 Major,	1 Lieutenant-Colonel,
1 Captain,	3 Captains,
2 Sergeants,	2 Lieutenants,
44 Rank and File.	2 Ensigns,
Since died of wounds,	3 Sergeants,
1 Captain,	2 Drummers,
1 Lieutenant,	127 Rank and File.
1 Ensign.	

Total killed and died of wounds, 51. Total wounded, deducting three since died of wounds, 137.

The American loss was killed, 84; wounded, 40.

Stephen Hempsted, one of the wounded survivors of the action, went to the state of Missouri, near St. Louis, in 1811. He published there a narrative of the battle on Groton Heights—correct in some things and very incorrect in others—and particularly so in the case of Colonel Nathan Gallup. In his narrative he says: "But a militia colonel was in the fort, and promised Colonel Ledyard that if he would hold out he would reinforce him in fifteen minutes with two or three hundred men. Colonel Ledyard agreed to send back a defiance upon the most solemn assurance of immediate succour. For this purpose Colonel ———— started, his men being then in sight; but he was no more seen, nor did he even attempt a diversion in our favor." Almost every person knew that Colonel Nathan Gallup was meant. He was at that time lieutenant-colonel of the 8th regiment of Connecticut Militia.

The true facts in the case are these. Colonel Ben Adam Gallup was in the fort previous to the action. Colonel Ledyard requested him to go back as far as Captain Belton's and urge on the men, but before he had time to return the enemy were so near that he could not re-enter the fort.

In 1782 Colonel McClallen, of Woodstock, was commander of New London harbor. At that time a court-martial was held for the trial of officers. Colonel Nathan Gallup came before said court as a prisoner, under six specific charges, from the whole of which he acquitted with honor and his certificate of acquittal signed by all the officers of the court, viz. the following:

Roger Newberry, of Hartford County, *President.*
Hezekiah Bissel, of Windham, *Judge Advocate.*
Joshua Downer, *Surgeon.*
Avery Downer, *Assistant Surgeon.*
Medical staff of said 8th regiment of Connecticut Militia.

When I look over the names inscribed on the tablets of the monument erected as a memorial of their heroism, language fails me to express my feelings. With many of them I was well acquainted, particularly with Captain Amos Staunton and his lieutenant, Henry Williams, both natives of Groton, and at that time home on furloughs from the army.

They went into the conflict as volunteers, left their wives and children and every thing near and dear to them, in defending the rights of their country. Can we and shall we, their descendants, pass over the memory of such patriotic men, and their invincible courage and fortitude be forgotten? No; let their heroism and valor be engraved on the tablets of our hearts and all that may follow us, and endure as long as the sun and the moon shall light the day and the night.

This narrative is this day finished with my own hand. I am 88 years and 5 months old.

AVERY DOWNER.

Preston, April 17th, 1851.

FROM

RIVINGTON'S ROYAL GAZETTE,

(NEW YORK.)

ON Thursday morning, the 6th inst., the fleet arrived
off New London harbor, where a part of the brave
though little army were sent to Groton, opposite New London, under command of Colonel Ayre, of the 40th regiment, to take possession of Fort Cressel, which commanded
not only the entrance of New London harbour, but the
mouth of the river Thames leading to Norwich. On the
appearance of the fleet five or six privateers lying in New
London harbour availed themselves of their oars and went
up said river; but before the rebels had an opportunity of
getting their valuable vessels out, General Arnold made it
necessary for them to look out for their personal safety. In
the meantime Colonel Ayre, with the detachment under
his command, landed within three miles of Fort Cressel,
and marched up with the spirit peculiar to the British nation; and though the country was so very rocky as to ren-
der it impossible for their artillery and howitzers to be
brought to co-operate with them, their thirst for glory was
such that as soon as they came to the skirt of a wood within
about a mile of the fort,[1] they sent an officer with a flag de-

---

[1] The British head-quarters that day were at the "Old Avery House"
—now demolished—situated about three-quarters of a mile south-east of
the fort, on the road running through the woods from Groton to Poquonoc. Here the soldiers gratified their love of mischief by wantonly
destroying the summer's dairy, breaking the furniture, throwing the old
clock out through the window, and badly frightening, by threats of ab-
duction, a young mother left with her infant alone in the house.

manding an immediate surrender, with a threat that if the demand was not complied with, it would be stormed five minutes after the return of the flag.

The officer who carried it advanced to a little eminence before the fort, and was met by an officer from it, who requested to know his errand, his rank, &c.; but being told that his business was with the commanding officer of the fort, he returned. After a considerable time on that spot the GREAT COMMANDER appeared, accompanied by another officer; the former having asked the gentleman who demanded the surrender his rank, and being satisfied that he was a captain in the British service, desired him to talk with and make his demand known to the captain who accompanied him, that he was of equal rank, and that for his "own part he was Colonel Ledyard, commanding officer of the fort."

The doughty rebel captain, being informed of the demand, told the officer that Colonel Ledyard had determined, as the fort was well garrisoned, and in every respect in a proper state of defence, he was under no apprehension of bad consequences, and would defend the fort to the last extremity.

The detention of the flag had tired the patience of not only Colonel Ayre, but of every officer and private centinel under his command, and on its return the order was given for an immediate storm, which was immediately put in execution. When the troops entered there was before the fort (which was regularly built with stone, mounting on the upper battery three, and on the lower eight pieces of cannon, with bastions at each corner, with guns to reach each curtain line,) a chevaux-de-frize, and a ditch of seven feet in depth on each square, with stockades on the sides next the fort. When the troops got into the ditch the rebels struck the flag and ceased firing,[1] until they pulled out some of the stakes and mounted on the range, when the rebels began to play their guns from the bastions, and attempted to defend their ramparts, but the valor of our troops prevailed, and the rebels fled into the casemates of the fortress, and some of them fired through the loop-holes; but the doors being burst open they were compelled to beg mercy, which being the darling attribute of Britons even to a fault, they spared the catiffs.   It is said the number of men in Fort Cressel was 250; forty of them being wounded were admitted to their parole, about 70 were sent prisoners on board the fleet, and the residue reaped the **BLESSED** fruits of their obstinacy.[2]   In the town of Groton the wounded, with the women and children, were put in two houses used as hospitals, and the town, together with two magazines, intirely demolished.   At New London the magazines, the town, and all the shipping in the harbour, were instantly reduced to ashes, but the number of killed, wounded, and prisoners taken, we have not yet been able to learn.

The breast of every honest loyalist can not help emotions of joy on finding that the most detestable nest of pirates on the continent have at last (the measure of their iniquity being full) attracted the notice of his Excellency the commander-in-chief.   The quantity of European and

---

[1] This incident is referred to in no other account, and is, without doubt, untrue.   Had such been the fact Arnold would not have allowed to pass unnoticed a circumstance in which there would have been so much palliation for the massacre which followed.

[2] This malignant report was, without doubt, furnished by Captain Beckwith, who was the officer sent to demand the surrender.   He accompanied Lord Dalrymple as bearer of dispatches from Arnold to Sir Henry Clinton, and arrived in New York some time before the remainder of the expedition, or any person who could have given so detailed an account in time to publish so soon after the battle.

West India goods in New London were immense. All their store-houses being full several cargoes were deposited in barns. It was, in fact, the magazine of America, and the blow now given will effect the sensitive nerves of every staunch rebel on the continent. Before the troops left the forts at New London, and Fort Cressel at Groton, they beat off the trunions of the cannon and spiked them up.

BRIGADIER-GENERAL ARNOLD'S REPORT

TO

SIR HENRY CLINTON.

PLUM ISLAND, Sept. 8th, 1781.

SIR: I have the honor to inform your Excellency that the transports with the detatchment of troops under my orders, anchored on the Long Island shore on the 5th inst., at 2 P. M., about ten leagues from New London, and having made some necessary arrangements, weighed anchor at 7 P. M., and stood for New London with a fair wind. At one o'clk the next morning we arrived off the harbor, when the wind suddenly shifted to the northward, and it was 9 o'clk before the transports could beat in.

At 10 o'clk the troops, in two divisions and in four debarkations, were landed, one on each side of the harbor, about three miles from New London, that on the Groton side consisting of the 40th and 54th regiments, and the 3d battalion of the New Jersey Volunteers, with a detachment of Yaggers and artillery, were under command of Lieutenant-Colonel Eyre.

The division on the New London side consisted of the 38th regiment,[1] the Loyal Americans,[2] the American Legion

---

[1] This was Sir Robert Pigot's regiment, but it is not known whether he was with the expedition. The uniform was red faced with yellow.— *Caulkins.*

[2] Colonel Beverly Robinson's regiment.

Refugees, and a detachment of 60 Yaggers,[1] who were immediately, on their landing, put in motion, and at 11 o'clock, being within half a mile of Fort Trumbull, which commands New London harbor, I detatched Captain Millet with four companies of the 38th regiment to attack the fort, who was joined on his march by Captain Frink with one company of the American Legion. At the same time I advanced with the remainder of the division west of Fort Trumbull, on the road to the town to attack a redoubt which had kept up a brisk fire on us for some time, but which the enemy evacuated on our approach. In this work we found 6 pieces of cannon mounted and 2 dismounted. Soon after I had the pleasure to see Captain Millet march into Fort Trumbull under a shower of grapeshot from a number of cannon which the enemy had turned upon him; and I have the pleasure to inform your Excellency that by the sudden attack and determined bravery of the troops the fort was carried with the loss of 4 or 5 men killed and wounded. Captain Millet had orders to leave one company in Fort Trumbull, to detatch one to the redoubt we had taken, and to join me with the other two companies.

No time on my part was lost in gaining the town of New London. We were opposed by a small body of the enemy with one field-piece, who were so hard pressed that they were obliged to leave the piece, which being iron was spiked and left.[2]

As soon as the enemy was alarmed in the morning we

---

[1] Hessian Light Infantry. They wore a dark green uniform with bright red trimmings.—*Caulkins.*

[2] This gun was a six-pounder, situated on Manwaring's Hill, and was used for the purpose of firing salutes; but on this occasion three or four resolute persons discharged it upon the enemy as they came down Town Hill, and then fled.—*Caulkins.*

could perceive that they were very busily employed in
bending sails, and endeavouring to get their privateers and
other ships into Norwich River out of our reach; but the
wind being small and the tide against them they were
obliged to anchor again.   From information I received before and after landing I had reason to believe that Fort
Griswold, on Groton side, was very incomplete; and I was
assured, (by friends to government,[1]) after my landing, that
there were only 20 or 30 men in the fort, the inhabitants in
general being on board their ships, and busy in saving their
property.   On taking possesion of Fort Trumbull I found
the enemy's ships would escape unless we could possess ourselves of Fort Griswold; I therefore dispatched an officer
to Lieutenant-Colonel Eyre with the intelligence I had received, and requested him to make an attack upon the fort
as soon as possible, at which time I expected the howitzer
was up, and would have been made use of.   On my gaining a height of ground in the rear of New London, from
which I had a good prospect of Fort Griswold,[2] I found it
much more formidable than I expected, or than I had
formed an idea of, from the information I had before received.   I observed at the same time that the men who
had escaped from Fort Trumbull had crossed the river in
boats and had thrown themselves into Fort Griswold; and
a favorable wind springing up about this time, the enemy's
ships were escaping up the river, notwithstanding the fire

---

[1] Arnold dined that day at the house of *his friend,* James Tilley, on
Bank Street; but the hospitality of the latter did not prevent the destruction of his buildings.   Before they arose from the table the roof over
their heads was in flames, though, we must suppose, from accidental ig-
nition or misapprehension of orders, as Tilley is said to have been well
known as a *"friend to government."*

[2] The old burial-ground.   It is said by old citizens that Arnold's point
of observation was the Winthrop tomb, whence he directed the movements of his soldiers in the destruction of the town.

from Fort Trumbull and a 6 pounder which I had with me. I immediately dispatched a boat with an officer to Lieutenant-Colonel Eyre to countermand my first order to attack the fort, but the officer arrived a few minutes too late. Lieutenant-Colonel Eyre had sent Captain Beckwith to demand the surrender of the fort, which was peremptorily refused, and the attack had commenced. After a most obstinate defence of near forty minutes the fort was carried by the superior bravery and perseverance of the battalions. The attack was judicious and spirited, and reflects the highest honor on the officers and troops engaged, who seemed to vie with each other in being first in danger.

The troops approached on three sides of the work, which was a square with flankers, made a lodgement in the ditch, and under a heavy fire which they kept up on the works effected a second lodgement upon the fraizing, which was attended with great difficulty, as only a few pickets could be forced out or broken in a place, and was so high that the soldiers could not ascend without assisting each other. Here the coolness and bravery of the troops was very conspicuous, as the first who ascended the fraize were obliged to silence a nine-pounder, which infiladed the place upon which they stood until a sufficient body had collected to enter the works, which was done with fixed bayonets through the embrasures, where they were opposed with great obstinacy by the garrison with long spears.[1] On this occasion I have to regret the loss of Major Montgomery, who was killed by a spear on entering the enemy's works;[2] also of Ensign Willock, of the 40th, who was killed in the attack. Three other officers of the same regiment were also wounded. Lieutenant-Colonel Eyre[3] and three other

---

[1] Probably boarding-pikes, used on board naval vessels in close combat.

[2] Montgomery was killed by a powerful negro named Jordan Freeman.

[3] Colonel Eyre is reported to have subsequently died on board the fleet.

officers of the 54th regiment were also wounded, but I have
the satisfaction to inform your Excellency that they are all
in a fair way to recover.   Lieutenant-Colonel Eyre, who
behaved with great gallantry, having received his wound
near the works, and Major Montgomery being killed immediately after, the command devolved on Major Bromfield,
whose behaviour on this occasion does him great honor.
Lieutenant-Colonel Buskirk, with the New Jersey Volunteers and artillery, being the second debarkation, came up
soon after the works were carried, having been retarded by
the roughness of the country.   I am much obliged to this
gentleman for his exertions, although the artillery did not
arrive in time.

I have annexed a Return of the killed and wounded, by
which your Excellency will observe that our loss, though
very considerable, is very short of the Enemy's, who lost
most of their officers, among whom was their commander,
Colonel Ledyard.   Eighty-five men were found dead in
Fort Griswold, and sixty wounded, most of them mortally.
Their loss on the opposite side must have been considerable,
but can not be ascertained.   I believe we have about 70
prisoners besides the wounded who were paroled.   Ten or
twelve of the Enemy's ships were burned, among them
three or four armed vessels, and one loaded with Naval
Stores.   An immense quantity of European and West India Goods were found in the stores; among the former the
cargo of the Hannah, Captain Watson, from London, lately
captured by the Enemy, the whole of which was burnt with
the stores, which proved to contain a large Quantity of
Powder unknown to us.   The explosion of the Powder
and change of wind soon after the stores were fired communicated the flames to that part of the Town, which was,
notwithstanding every effort to prevent it, unfortunately de-

stroyed.[1] Upwards of 50 pieces of Iron Cannon were destroyed in the different Works, (exclusive of the Guns of the Ships,) a particular return of which I can not do myself the Honor to transmit to your Excellency at this time.

A very considerable Magazine of Powder, and Barracks to contain 300 men, were found in Fort Griswold, which Captain Lemoine, of the Royal Artillery, had my positive directions to destroy. An attempt was made by him, but unfortunately failed. He had my orders to make a second attempt. The reason why it was not done Captain Lemoine will have the honor to explain to your Excellency.[2] I should be wanting in justice to the gentlemen of the Navy did I omit to acknowledge that on this expedition I have received every possible aid from them. Captain Beazly has made every exertion to assist our operations, and not only gave up his cabin to the sick and wounded officers, but furnished them with every assistance and refreshment

---

[1] There is the greatest absurdity in this part of the narrative, for in many instances where houses were situated at a great distance from any stores, and contained nothing but household furniture, they were set on fire, notwithstanding the earnest cries and entreaties of the women and children in them, who were threatened with being burnt up in their houses if they did not instantly leave them. Indeed two houses were bought off for ten pounds each after an officer, who appeared to be a captain, had ordered them fired, which was the sum proposed by the officer, upon condition, however, that he should not be made known; and where the houses were not burnt they were chiefly plundered of all that could be carried off. At the Harbor's Mouth the houses of poor fishermen were stripped of their furniture of every kind, the poor people having nothing left but the clothes they had on.—*Connecticut Gazette, September 21st, 1781.*

*   *   *   *   *   *   *   *

[2] *Extract from General Orders of the 25th of September,* 1781.— The commander-in-chief informs the army that Captain Lemoine, of the Royal Artillery, has explained to his satisfaction the reasons that prevented his carrying into execution the orders of Brigadier-General Arnold on the 6th of September, 1781.   CLINTON.

10

his ship afforded. Lord Dalrymple will have the honour to deliver my dispatches. I beg leave to refer your Excellency to his Lordship for the particulars of our operations on the New London side. I feel myself under great obligations to him for his exertions upon the occasion. Captain Beckwith, who was extremely serviceable to me, returns with his Lordship. His spirited conduct in the attack of Fort Griswold does him great honor, being one of the first officers who entered the work. I beg leave to refer your Excellency to him for the particulars of our operations on that side, and to say I have the highest opinion of his abilities as an officer. I am greatly indebted to Captain Stapleton (who acted as Major of Brigade) for his spirited conduct and assistance; in particular on the attack on Fort Trumbull, and his endeavour to prevent plundering,[1] (when the public stores were burnt,) and the destruction of private buildings. The officers and troops in general behaved with the greatest intrepidity and firmness. I have the honor to be, with the greatest respect, your Excellency's most obedient and most humble servt., **B. ARNOLD.**

RETURN OF KILLED AND WOUNDED.

1 Major, 1 Ensign, 2 Sergeants, and 44 Rank and File, killed; 1 Lieutenant-Colonel, 3 Captains, 2 Lieutenants, 2 Ensigns, 8 Sergeants, 2 Drummers, and 127 Rank and File, wounded. Of the wounded officers 1 Captain, 1 Lieutenant, and 1 Ensign, are since dead.

JOHN STAPLETON,
Captain and Acting Major of Brigade.

---

[1] It was afterwards well understood that most of the spoil and havoc in private houses was the work of a few worthless vagrants of the town, who prowled in the wake of the invader, hoping, in the general confusion, not to be detected.—*Caulkins.*

RETURN OF ORDNANCE, AMMUNITION, &c.,

Taken this day in Fort Griswold and its dependencies, by a detatchment of His Majesty's troops under the command of Brigadier-General Arnold, on an expedition to Connecticut, viz., in Fort Griswold:

ORDNANCE MOUNTED ON CARRIAGES.

Garrison 18 pounders,	1	12 pounders,	14
9 "	2	6 "	1
4 "	1	3 "	1
Travelling 12 "	1	4 "	2
		Total,	23

In the Fleche, 6 pounders, 1

ORDNANCE MOUNTED ON TRAVELLING CARRIAGES.

4 pounders,	3	12 pounders,	2
6 "	4		—
		Total,	9
Total of Iron Ordnance,			35
Pikes,	80	Musquets, French,	106

ROUND SHOT.

18 pounders,	1680	12 pounders,	2100
9 "	290	6 "	100
4 "	200	3 "	40

GRAPE, STANDS OF.

18 pounders,	230	12 pounders,	340
9 "	75	6 "	70
4 "	90	3 "	75

CARTRIDGES PAPER FILLED.

18 pounders,   12   12 pounders,   23   9 pounders,   8
6   "   4   4   "   14   3   "   6

Musket Cartridges, 10,000.
Powder corned, 150 wt.
1 Garrison Spare carriage, 12 pounder.
1 Gyn Triangle compleat; Stores for the Laboratory, &c.,
&c., &c.

J. LEMOINE,
Captain of Artillery.

BETSEY, SLOOP, NEW LONDON HARBOUR, 6TH SEPT., 1781.

Return of ordnance found and spiked by a detatchment
of the army under the command of Brigadier-General Arnold, on the New London side, 6th Sept., 1781:

Iron 18 pounders mounted in Fort Trumbull,	12
Iron 6 pounders mounted in Fort Trumbull,	3
Iron 12 or 9 pounders mounted at Fort Folly,[1]	6
Iron 12 or 9 pounders dismounted,	2
Iron 12 pounders on the road to New London,	1
	24

A Quantity of ammunition and stores of different kinds
were destroyed in the Magazine at Fort Trumbull, and the
Meeting House at New London.

WILLIAM H. HORNDON,
First Lieutenant Regiment Royal Artillery.

---

[1] This was known to the Americans by the kindred name of Fort Nonsense.   It occupied the extreme height of Town Hill, where now stands
the residence of F. M. Hale, Esq.   When the excavation was being
made for the cellar, several relics of its revolutionary history in the shape
of round and grape shot, deeply eaten by rust, were exhumed.

LIEUTENANT-COLONEL   UPHAM

TO

GOVERNOR FRANKLIN,[1] OF NEW JERSEY,

DATED SEPTEMBER 13TH, 1781.

IMMEDIATELY on receipt of yours by Capt. Camp I made every preparation consistent with the necessary secresy to furnish as many Refugees for the proposed expedition as could be spared from the garrison.

My first care was to put a supply of provisions on board the vessels. I talked of an expedition, and proposed to go myself, nor could I do more until the fleet appeared in sight. Major Hubbil was too unwell to go with me; I therefore left him to take charge of the fort, and with as much dispatch as possible embarked one hundred Loyalists, exclusive of a sufficient number of men to man the two armed sloops. With these we joined the fleet in season to prevent the least delay.

By the enclosed arrangement you see we had the honor to be included in the first division, and I have the pleasure to add we were the first on shore.

We advanced on the right of the whole to a height at a small distance from the shore, where we were ordered to

---

[1] This worthy had recently returned from his rural quarters in Litchfield jail, where he, with Mayor Mathews, of New York, was confined, in 1776, by the committee "for inquiring into and detecting conspiracies." —*Hollister.*

cover the 38th regiment from a wood on our right until the second division came up.

We were then ordered to change our position from the right to the left at the distance of two hundred yards from the main body.

This alteration derived its propriety from the circumstance of the rebels having gone over to the left, from an apprehension of being too much crowded between our troops and the river on their left. Thus arranged we proceeded to the town of New London, constantly skirmishing with rebels, who fled from hill to hill, and from stone fences which intersected the country at small distances.[1] Having reached the southerly part of the town the general requested me to take possession of the hill north of the meeting-house, where the rebels had collected, and which they seemed resolved to hold. We made a circle to the left, and soon gained the ground in contest.

Here we had one man killed and one wounded. This height being the outpost was left to us and the Yägers. Here we remained, exposed to a constant fire from the rebels on the neighboring hills and from the fort on the Groton side, until the last was carried by the British troops. We took the same route in our return as in going up, equally exposed, though not so much annoyed. Every thing required was cheerfully undertaken, and spiritedly effected by the party I had the honor to command.

A small party from Vanalstine's Post joined us, which increased my command to 120. They landed and returned

---

[1] Colonel Upham's command defiled through Cape Ann Street and Lewis Lane, and set fire to the house of Pickett Latimer, on the old Colchester road, now Vauxhall Street.—*Caulkins.* This was the first building destroyed; in it were the goods of the inhabitants, who removed them to it from the central portion of the town, as being a place of greater safety.

with us, and behaved exceedingly well.   The Armed Vessels Association and Colonel Martin went close into the shore, and covered the landing on the New London side. At the request of the general I furnished boats to land forty of the troops on the Groton side.   Captains Gardener and Thomas would have gladly gone up to the town, but were not permitted.

SIR HENRY CLINTON'S

GENERAL ORDERS.

BRIGADIER-GENERAL ARNOLD having reported
to the commander-in-chief the success of the expedition, under his direction, against New London on the 6th
inst., His Excellency has the pleasure of signifying to the
army the high sense he entertains of the very distinguished
merit of the corps employed upon that service.

But whilst he draws the greatest satisfaction from the ardor of the troops which enabled them to carry by assault
a work of such great strength as Fort Griswold is represented to be, he can not but lament with the deepest concern the heavy loss in officers and men sustained by the
40th and 54th regiments, who had the honor of the attack;
and as no words can do justice to the discipline and spirit
which they shewed on that occasion, His Excellency can
only request they will not fail to represent their conduct to
their sovereign in the most honorable terms. The commander-in-chief begs leave to express his obligation to
Brigadier-General Arnold for his very spirited conduct on
the occasion; and he assures that general officer that he
took every precaution in his power to prevent the destruction of the town, which is a misfortune that gives him
much concern. His Excellency also feels himself greatly
indebted to all the officers of the Regular and Provincial
Corps which accompanied him on that service, but more
particularly to Lieutenant-Colonel Eyre, Major Bromfield,

and Captain Millet, who commanded the attack, and Lord Dalrymple, Captains Beckwith and Stapleton, of whose very able assistance and distinguished gallantry the brigadier makes the most honorable mention.

The commander-in-chief has likewise the greatest pleasure in taking this public occasion of signifying to the army how much they are indebted to the humanity and benevolence of Captain Beazley, of His Majesty's Ship Amphion, to whose very friendly and generous assistance many of the wounded officer and men are most probably indebted for their lives.

FRED. MACKENZIE, *D. A. General.*

COURT-MARTIAL.

AN extract from the proceedings of a general Court-Martial, beginning and held at New London and Groton, in the state of Connecticut, on the 20th day of August, Anno Domini 1782, by warrant and order of His Excellency the Captain-General of the said state, of which Brigadier-General Roger Newberry was President,

In which the following crimes and charges were exhibited at said Court, and by them with the proofs assenting the same were duly heard and considered, after which the sentences of said Court-martial were as follows:

Jonathan Latimer, Colonel of the 3d regiment, for breach of military law in not leading his regiment forward, and preventing the enemy from sacking and burning the town of New London, on the 6th day of September, A. D. 1781. From this charge he was acquitted with honor.

Nathan Gallup, Esq., Lieutenant-Colonel of the 8th regiment, came prisoner before the court, when the following charge was exhibited against him, viz: That whereas, on the 6th day of September, A. D. 1781, (the day on which the garrison and fortress standing in said Groton was attacked and stormed by a detachment of the British army; the inhabitants of said Groton massacred; their houses burnt and their property plundered;) that he then holding and sustaining the aforesaid office and a commission thereto in said regiment, was shamefully negligent in his military duty, and guilty of acting a cowardly part when called to and in actual service.

1st. In not supporting the garrison in said fort with succour, which was in his power, and by him had been specially engaged to the commandant for his encouragement in defending it, and in making no diversion upon the enemy before the storm in favor of the garrison.

2dly. In suffering the militia to remain strolling and unembodied upon the hills, in fair view of the enemy when they were marching up to attack the fort.

3dly. In not falling upon and attacking the enemy at the favorable moment of their re-embarkation, which movement of the enemy was said to be well known to him.

4thly. In not attempting to prevent the burning of houses and other buildings of the inhabitants in Groton, done by scattering parties of the enemy.

5thly. In not preventing the wanton plundering of property belonging to the inhabitants, done by the militia and others in the houses which escaped the conflagration, and elsewhere in said town after the storm of said garrison and the burning done by the enemy.

And 6thly. In not preserving the public stores in the fort after the evacuation by the enemy, but suffering them to be embezzled and plundered; all contrary to the rules and regulations for preserving order and good government among the militia of said state, and unbecoming an officer.

Sentence.—The court, upon due consideration of the whole matter before them, are unanimously of opinion that Lieutenant-Colonel Nathan Gallup is not guilty of neglect of duty or of cowardly behaviour, as charged against him. He, therefore, by the Court is acquitted with honor.

Captain John Morgan, of the 3d regiment, was adjudged guilty of neglect of duty and unofficer like behaviour, and sentenced to be suspended during the present war with Great Britain.

Captain Ebenezer Witter, of the 8th regiment, was charged with being concerned in plundering public property at Fort Griswold. The court found him not guilty of plundering, but that he acted a very imprudent part in ordering the gun carried to his house, and the court ordered him to return the said gun to the commanding officer at Fort Griswold.

Captain Thomas Wheeler and Lieutenant John Williams, of the 8th regiment, were charged with plundering in a wanton and shameful manner the goods of the inhabitants of Groton on the day of the battle.

The court found them guilty, and sentenced them to be cashiered, and be disabled in future from holding or sustaining any military commission in this state, and that they pay the expenses of their trial in equal parts.

Daniel Latimer, Ensign of a company of militia in the 3d regiment, was charged with being negligent of his duty in not seasonably forwarding intelligence to his colonel of the expected approach and attack of the enemy. He was found not guilty, and was therefore acquitted.

Zabdiel Rogers, Esq., Colonel of the 20th regiment, was called upon to answer to the charge of remaining inactive upon the 6th day of September. The sentence was not guilty, and acquitted with honor.

Joseph Harris,[1] Jun., Esq., Lieutenant-Colonel of the 3d

---

[1] Lieutenant-Colonel Harris resided on the Town Hill road, nearly opposite Fort Nonsense. He is alluded to by John Hempstead and Jonathan Brooks in their narratives in not very complimentary terms. He appears to have been the only regimental officer of the 3d who resided in the immediate vicinity of hostilities that day. In the Connecticut Gazette of May 2d, 1783, he replied to the finding of the Court, and excused himself from the charge, taking up each specification in its order,

regiment, came prisoner before the Court, when the following charges were exhibited against him: That on the day when the British burned the town he was shamefully negligent in his military duty, and guilty of acting a cowardly part.

1st. In not notifying his chief colonel of the enemy's approach.

2d. In not opposing their entrance into the town.

3d. In not supporting a part of said regiment when in battle at the north part of the town, which he was requested to, but shamefully refused to do.

4th. In allowing the militia to remain strolling and unembodied upon the hill in sight of the enemy. And

5thly. In not falling upon and attacking the enemy on their retreat.

The court unanimously gave it as their opinion that Lieutenant-Colonel Harris has been and is a worthy member of society, and a good citizen in private life, *but not* suitably qualified for military service; that he was not guilty of any neglect of duty on said 6th of September from enmity or disaffection to the independence of the American states; but the Court are unanimously of opinion that he was and is guilty of the matter charged against him in the four first articles of charge, and also are of opinion that he is guilty in the fifth, and that the whole are proved and supported against him; therefore the Court gives sentence against the said Harris, that he be cashiered as being a person unsuitable to sustain the aforesaid office.

Warham Williams was found guilty of taking and holding three guns, and was remanded to the civil authority to be dealt with.

---

and commenting at length upon it. Some of the arguments brought forward by him in support of his innocence are more ingenious than logical; and, as viewed at this late day, his conclusions are strained and far drawn.

Benajah Leffingwell, Major of the 20th regiment, was charged with neglect of duty on the day of battle, from which charge he was acquitted.

The findings of the Court are approved by the Captain-General, and by his command are made public.

Signed, **HEZEKIAH BISSEL,**
Judge Advocate of said Court-Martial.

FROM THE

CONNECTICUT ARCHIVES,

REVOLUTIONARY WAR, VOL. XXII., DOC. 337.

To Col. McClellen, Commandant at the Pofts of New
London & Groton.

We, Inhabitants of N. London, beg leave to represent
our fears & apprehenfions for the fafety of faid Pofts
through the infuing fummer;—from the defencelefs ftate of
the Garrifons, &c., and from the growing object of this
Town, by the indufterous inhabitants erecting a number of
Houfes & Stores, in order to aid and affift y⁰ fpirited Gentlemen in the country, in fitting & equiping their Privateers,
which are now numerous & formidable; Several Prizes are
brought in, & great wealth may be foon expected, all which
is as likely to provoke the narrow pitiful revenge of our
daftardly enemies, to diftroy us this fumer, as laft.

Every year fince the commincement of the war, this
Town has been alarmed with envafions, the confequences
has always been that great numbers of melitia are called
from their labours & fent in upon us, on fo fhort a notice
yᵗ it was impoffible for them to be compleatly equiped;
and have been detained here during a long fummer, greatly
to their private lofs—the public, and the immediate ex-
pence of the State, which has been much greater then if
we had proper Garrisons & Matrofs Companys ftationed
here, without anfwering any real means of defennce; and
at the fame time the inhabitants of the Town are equally

fufferers from undifciplined melitia. And from the late attack at this Place it was fo evident that the melitia were
not, and could not be here in time to be of any fervice,
that it needs no obfervation to the contrary.

To remedy which & to fecure thefe Pofts we fubmit it
to you as our opinion, that

Fort Grifwold fhould be garrifoned with at leaft one hundred & fifty good men—that the Fort be provided with
200 fmall arms & fufficient number of cartriges & as many
pikes for ufe of volunteers, who may be called in as they
are many tranfient perfons & fuch y^t are unable to equip
themfelves; and that on the firing of the alarm guns, or
notice given, it fhall be the immediate duty of the neigh-
bouring militia to march into the defence of the s^d Fort on
pain of nothing fhort of fuffering the penalty of the Law,
& that to be made corporeal, let the delinquent be officer
or private; and as foon as the alarm is over to be difmiffed.

That their be a Matrofs Company raifed fufficient to
man what Field Peices we have on N. L. fide & thofe at
Norwich, & to be compleatly furnifhed with horfes, &c.,
and ftationed in the Fort on Town Hill; & be provided
with fome fmall arms, as many volunteers will run to their
affiftance in time of alarm. That the melitia in the neigh-
bourhood be ordered in as on Groton fide. The Garrifon
at Fort Trumbull may be fmall, & to quit it on the actual
approach of the enemy & to retire to the defence of the
field peices or Fort Grifwold.

That no veffells on the firing of the alarm guns, that are
in the harbour be permitted to be removed, excepting fmall
craft, but by order & direction of the Commandant.

That after ye alarm, or actual fervice is over their fhall
be an enquiry into the conduct of every officer & private
& all others ordered on duty, & on failure of duty to be
punifhed according to the nature of the offence, which pun-

ifhment ought to be corporeal. For men will not regard
fines when their property is at ftake. Common rank & file
will delight in fuch a militia law. We obferve further it
is our opinion, if the late worthy Col. Ledyard (whom we
fincerely lament) had only fifty good men in the Fort under
his abfolute command, he with them might have empreff'd
& compelled into its defence two or three hundred feamen
& others, which had deferted from Privateers & fhipping in
order to plunder. But inftead of this he was as a man
without hands, and could get none into the fort only by
perfuation. He gave out his pofitive orders for all feamen
to repair over to the Fort. He fired upon the fhiping to
ftop them from runing away. But he was neglected with
impunity. He was difobcy'd becaufe the laws are not ad-
equate for the punifhment of difobedience of orders. They
ought to be exceedingly fevere when called out into action.
And if men of Spirit who run to the defence of any poft
in time of danger are to be unfupported & facrificed by
their neighbours, (who are at liberty to take care of their
effects, keep out of danger & not liable to corporeal punifhment,) who will run the rifque in future. Wee make
bold to fay, had fome Gentlemen neglected their duty y^e
6th Spr. laft they would have faved thoufands of their
property.

If a fmall cruifing boat could be alowed to the Garrifon,
it might be an encouragement to inlifting their men & alfo
obtaining intelligence the profits to be theirs.

If all or any of the above facts & reprefentations fhould
agree with your obfervation & opinion, we would requeft
you to lay the fame before His Excellency & Council—
urging their immediate attention, as a great faving to the
State & equal or better fecurity then the ufial mode. Who
we make no doubt will do all in their power to fill up the
Garrifon at Fort Grifwold & to forward the beft plan of de-

12

fence, and to ufe all their influance in the next General
Affembly to have fuch Military Laws paffed as will be
neceffary in alarm & invafions.

　　　　　　We are with efteem & refpect,

　　　　　　　　　Sir,

　　　　　　　　　　　Your moft Hum^e Serv's,

New London April 22^d 1782.

G. Saltonftall,	Thos. Shaw,
Timo. Green,	John Defhon,
Marvin Wait,	Amafa Larnard,
Pember Calkings,	Edward Hallam,
Wint. Saltonftall,	Michael Melally,
David Mumford,	Guy Richards, Junr,
	Simon Wolcott,
	James Angel,

Col. McClellen,
　　Prefent.

CONNECTICUT ARCHIVES,

Revolutionary War, Vol. XXII., Doc. 338.

Report of Committee de Fort at New London, May 1782.

We Your Honours Com^tee appointed to take into confideration the reprefentation made by a number of Gentlemen from New London, refpecting the Defence of the
Poft at N. London, &c., beg leave to report,

　That the Governuour and Council of Safety be and they
are defired, to raife a fufficient fum out of ye provifions on

hand (or loan as may be) to pay the 40*s*. bounty ordered to the foldiers that may engage in the forts at N. London & Groton provided by act of Affembly in Jany laft (and that 48 matroffes be raifed in addition to the number already ordered by act of Affembly, and that the fame pay & bounty be given them as the other before provided for) & that in the mean time His Excellency order fuch numbers of militia to man the Garrison untill a fuitable number may be enlifted, and that 200 Arms be provided & fent to the care of the commander at that Poft for the ufe of the fame.

All which is fubmitted by your Hum^e Serv^{ts},

Comfort Sage, ⎫
Edwd Ruffel, ⎭ c^{ee}

In the Lower Houfe.

The foregoing Report of Committee is accepted and approved, fo far as to include the word *laft* in the 12th line of the Report from the top, with addition (viz..) "provided faid foldiers do not live within fix miles from s^d Forts," next after the word *laft* aforefaid. And that a Bill, &c.

Teft, Increafe Mofeley, Clerk, P. T.

Concurr'd in the upper Houfe.

Teft, George Wyllys, Secret.

CONNECTICUT ARCHIVES,

REVOLUTIONARY WAR, VOL. XXII., DOC. 339.

New London, 1ˢᵗ June, 1782.

Sir:

Since writing the inclofed have feen Col° M°Clannan, he defires me to inform your Excellency that the Troops at this Poft under his command will now not make two Relieves, he is diftreff'd to fupply the Forts and Prifon Ship.

I think it my duty to inform your Excellency that there is a large number of veffels here, & other intereft, befide the Alliance Frigate, & fcarce any men to defend the Forts at Groton & this Town, your Excellency will pleafe excufe the freedom I take in giving fuch information as [it] refpects the publick—

I am with fentiments of Rea[l] Efteem,
      Your Excellencys very obed' Serv',
                              Tho' Mumford.

Superfcribed,
      Publick Service,
      His Excellency Governor Trumbull,
                        Hartford.

In dorfo.

In the Lower Houfe.

Col. Sage, Col. Ruffell & Maj' Hilhoufe appointed to take into confideration this Letter & Addreff of fundry Gentlemen of New London to Col. M°Clallen of the 22ᵈ April ult & laid before the Houfe, both refpecting the Defence of the Pofts of N. London & Groton and what ought to be done to report by bill or otherwife.

                    Teft Jedediah Strong, Clerk.

NAMES OF THE HEROES

WHO FELL AT FORT GRISWOLD,

SEPTEMBER 6TH, 1781.

GROTON.

Colonel William Ledyard,
David Avery, Esq.,
Captain John Williams,
Captain Simeon Allyn,
Captain Samuel Allyn,
Captain Elisha Avery,
Captain Amos Stanton,[1]
Captain Elijah Avery,
Captain Hubbard Burrows,
Captain Youngs Ledyard,
Captain Nathan Moore,[2]
Lieutenant Joseph Lewis,
Lieutenant Ebenezer Avery,
Lieutenant Henry Williams,
Lieutenant Patrick Ward,
Ensign John Lester,
Ensign Daniel Avery,
Sergeant John Stedman,[3]
Sergeant Solomon Avery,
Sergeant Jasper Avery,
Sergeant Ezekiel Bailey,[4]
Sergeant Rufus Hurlburt,

Sergeant Christopher Avery,[5]
Sergeant Eldridge Chester,
Sergeant Nicholas Starr,
Corporal Edward Mills,[6]
Corporal Luke Perkins, Jr.,[7]
Corporal Andrew Billings,
Corporal Simeon Morgan,
Corporal Nathan Sholes,[8]
Daniel Chester,
Thomas Avery,
David Palmer,
Sylvester Walworth,[9]
Philip Covel,[10]
Jedediah Chester,[11]
David Seabury,[12]
Henry Woodbridge,
Christopher Woodbridge,
Elnathan Perkins,
Luke Perkins,
Elisha Perkins,
John Brown,[13]
John P. Babcock,

Nathan Adams,[14]
Wait Lester,
Samuel Hill,[15]
Joseph Moxley,
Thomas Starr, Jr.,
Moses Jones,
Belton Allyn,
Benadam Allyn,
Jonas Lester,[16]
John Billings,[17]
Thomas Minard,

Andrew Baker,
Joseph Wedger,[18]
Samuel Billings,[19]
Eliday Jones,[20]
Thomas Lamb,[21]
Frederick Chester,[22]
Daniel Davis,[23]
Daniel D. Lester[24],
Asa Perkins,
Simeon Perkins,
Solomon Tift.[25]

NEW LONDON.

Captain Adam Shapley,
Captain Peter Richards,
Lieut. Richard Chapman,
Benoni Kenson,[26]
James Comstock,
John Holt,

John Clark,
Jonathan Butler,[27]
William Bolton,[28]
William Comstock,[29]
Elias Coit,[30]
Barney Kinney.[31]

Captain Elias Henry Halsey, Long Island.[32]

STONINGTON.

Lieutenant Enoch Stanton,   Thomas Williams.
Sergeant Daniel Stanton,

SAYBROOK.

Daniel Williams,
Stephen Whittlesey.[34]

John Whittlesey,[33]

Sambo Latham, colored.[35]   Jordan Freeman, colored.[36]

NOTE.—The numerals annexed to a portion of the names in the above list refer to notes in the Appendix, in which is given all information gained by critical inquiry and research regarding those of the slain whose places of sepulture are uncertain, or undistinguished by inscribed monuments.

NAMES OF THE WOUNDED,

PAROLED AND LEFT AT HOME BY CAPTAIN BROMFIELD.

Captain William Latham, wounded in the thigh, Groton.
Captain Solomon Perkins, in the face, Groton.
Captain Edward Latham, in the body, Groton.
Lieutenant P. Avery, lost an eye, Groton.
Lieutenant Obadiah Perkins, in the breast, Groton.
Lieutenant William Starr, in the breast, Groton.
Ensign Charles Eldridge, in the knee, Groton.
Ensign Joseph Woodmancy, lost an eye, Groton.
Ensign Ebenezer Avery, in the head, Groton.
John Morgan, shot through the knee, Groton.
Sanford Williams, shot in the body, Groton.
John Daboll, shot in the head, Groton.
Samuel Edgecomb, Jr., in the hand, Groton.
Jabish Pendleton, in the hand, Groton.
Asahel Woodworth, in the neck, Groton.
Thomas Woodworth, in the leg, Groton.
Ebenezer Perkins, in the face, Groton.
Daniel Eldridge, in the neck and face, Groton.
Christopher Latham, in the body, Groton.
Christopher Eldridge, in the face, Groton.
Amos Avery, in the hand, Groton.
T. Woodworth, in the knee, Groton.
Frederick Wave, in the body, Groton.
Elisha Prior, in the arm, Groton.
Sergeant Daniel Stanton, in the body, Stonington.
Corporal Judd, shot in the knee, Hebron.
William Seymour, lost his leg, Hartford.
Samuel Stillman, arm and thigh, Saybrook.
Stephen Hempstead, arm and body, New London.
Tom Wansuc, (Pequot Indian,) bayonet stab in neck.

FORT GRISWOLD.

PROBABLY no feature in the theatre of the battle has changed so little as the old fort. It is substantially the same in size and outline as then. The barracks, magazine and platform of that day have decayed and fallen, but their sites are still plainly recognizable by the ruins. Along the east side of the parade three soil-covered mounds mark the location of the old barrack chimneys. In the south-west bastion is the ruined masonry of the magazine, near which stood the flag-staff. Along the west side are still seen the stone foundations upon which rested the wood platform, and the well near the gate is the same to which, on that bloody day, the dying soldier in his fevered anguish wistfully turned, and vainly craved of the implacable Briton its cooling draught.

Near the centre of the parade are the ruins of a magazine constructed in 1798, when a war with France was considered imminent; and the coast fortifications, which had received but little attention since the peace of 1783, were put in a state of defense. In 1812–14 the old barracks were repaired, the ditch somewhat deepened, the parapets strengthened with fresh earth, and heavier ordnance mounted; but these guns and their carriages were a short time afterwards removed. In 1842 or '43 a commission from the War Department reported in favor of making this fort a permanent work; but the Mexican question, which was

then looming into view in the south-western horizon, caused
the abandonment of the project at that time, and it has
never since been revived. Aside from its commanding position this old fort would present to the military eye of fifty
years ago but small claims for offensive powers; but the
lessons of modern war have taught the engineer of to-day
that, mounted with improved artillery, the old sodded ruin
would be more capable of injury to an enemy, and far more
susceptible of defense, than the elaborate granite fortress
opposite. But, however strong and defiant it might be
made, let us hope the occasion for its proof will never
arise; that its grass-covered ramparts, once sanctified by
the blood of patriots, may never be torn by hostile shot—
never again be the scene of human conflict.

THE BATTLE MONUMENT.

In the year 1826 a number of gentlemen in Groton, feel-
ing that the tragic events occurring in the neighborhood in
1781 should be more properly commemorated, organized
as an association for the purpose of erecting a monument.
An application to the legislature for a charter was granted,
and a lottery in aid of the work was legalized by special
act. The corner-stone was laid September 6th of that
year, and on the 6th of September, 1830, it was dedicated
with imposing ceremonies.

In form it is an obelisk twenty-two feet square at the
base, and eleven feet at the top, resting on a die twenty-
four feet square, which in turn rests upon a base twenty-
six feet square. Its material is granite, quarried in the
neighborhood.

Its whole height is one hundred and twenty-seven feet,
and its summit, which is reached by a spiral stair-way of
one hundred and sixty stone steps, is two hundred and fifty-

seven feet above the waters of the bay. From this point a picture of sea and land of almost unrivaled beauty is presented, well repaying the visitor for the toil of ascent.

Upon a marble slab, on the west face over the entrance, is the following inscription:

———◆•◆———

This Monument

was erected under the patronage of the State of Connecticut, A. D. 1830, and in the 55th year of the Independence of the **U. S. A.**

In Memory of the *Brave Patriots*

who fell in the massacre at Fort Griswold near this spot on the 6th of September, A. D. 1781,

when the British under the command of

the *traitor Benedict Arnold,*

burnt the towns of New London & Groton, and spread desolation and woe throughout this region.

———•◆•———

Within the monument, upon the right of the entrance, is a marble tablet bearing the names of the heroes who fell on that bloody day. This was formerly on the south side of the monument, facing the fort; some years since, repairs becoming necessary, it was removed to the present location, and its place supplied with solid masonry. There was also above and connected with it, a slab bearing the following inscription, which was also removed at that time and never replaced:

"Zebulon and Naphtali were a people that jeoparded their lives unto the death in the high places of the field."

Judges, 5 Chap. 18 verse.

The *facsimile* of Colonel Ledyard's autograph, given below, was engraved from a letter addressed by him to the
selectmen of Lebanon, directing them to send to Norwich
Landing the stores they had collected for public service.
The letter is dated at New London, April 4th, 1781.

MONUMENTAL RECORDS.

THIS chapter was not comprehended in the plan of this little work as originally contemplated, but is rather an outgrowth from the interest excited in this direction by the compilation of the narratives, and has been adopted since that portion has been in press. The subject naturally follows, and will, it is thought, give additional interest if not value to the preceding narratives and reports, in which we see, amid the smoke of battle and in the frenzy of the death-struggle, the heroes whom we here follow to their quiet resting-places, and reading their homely epitaphs, seem in a measure to become personally acquainted with them.

A visit to the graves, near the scene of the battle, led to wider explorations in the many public and private cemeteries of Groton and adjacent townships. Nearly one hundred were visited, and the result, considering the general ignorance, and, it may also regretfully be said, the indifference of even their descendants regarding the sepulture of these brave men, was much more successful than was or could have been anticipated. Quite a large number of graves are known to have ever remained unprovided with engraved tablets, and of those which were properly so marked, many of the stones have fallen, and are now concealed by the heavy vegetable accumulations of years. Hence many, doubtless, were passed over undiscovered, even after extended inquiry and careful research. These neglected and forgotten memorials of the fathers' devotion to the cause of country and liberty are widely scattered through Groton and the neighboring towns, most frequently in obscure and lonely localities, sometimes hidden in the shade of heavy forest trees, and covered by dense undergrowth of noxious weeds and shrubs—the undisturbed home of the burrowing wild animal and noisome reptile.

On visiting these solitary places of interment, and reading from the monuments the rudely cut epitaphs which sometimes breathe a spirit of resignation and Christian hope, but far oftener that of defiant and fiery indignation, the visitor realizes more than ever before the extent of the desolation and woe spread throughout this region by the invasion of the traitor.

The lamented Frances Manwaring Caulkins, in addition to her many other historical and antiquarian labors, made quite extensive researches in this direction, the results of which she designed publishing at a future day, under the title of "The Stone Records of Groton."

On learning that the present work was in preparation, her brother, the Hon. Henry P. Haven, very generously proffered the editor the privilege of consulting her manuscripts, which have been of much assistance in preparing this difficult subject.

About four hundred and fifty yards south-east from the fort is the grave of Colonel Ledyard, whose name has been given to the cemetery, which was formerly known as that of Packer's Rock, from the high ledge upon its eastern border. In 1854 the state appropriated fifteen hundred dollars for the erection of a suitable memorial to the martyr. His remains, with those of his wife and children, were removed a few yards to the west near the centre of the ground, and a beautiful monument, cut from native granite, erected over his grave.

It is inclosed by an iron railing supported by posts ap-

propriately cast in the form of cannon. Within the inclosure are the remains of the slab of blue slate which originally marked the grave; it is now nearly destroyed, and the
inscription rendered illegible by the vandalism of the relic
hunter. On the west face of the monument, upon the
shaft, an unsheathed sabre is carved in relief; below, upon
the sub-base, in raised letters, is the name LEDYARD,
and on the die is the following inscription:

Sons of Connecticut
Behold this Monument and learn to emulate
the virtue valor and Patriotism of your ancestors.

The south face bears the following:

ERECTED IN 1854

By the State of Connecticut in remembrance of the
painful events that took place in this neighborhood
during the war of the Revolution;
It commemorates the Burning of New London,
the Storming of Groton Fort the Massacre of
the Garrison and the slaughter of Ledyard the
brave Commander of these posts who was slain
by the Conquerors with his own Sword.

He fell in the service of his country
Fearless of death and prepared to die.

On the north:

Copy of the Inscription on the Head-Stone originally erected over the Grave of Colonel Ledyard.

Sacred to the Memory of WILLIAM LEDYARD Efq'
Col'Commandant of the Garrifoned pofts of New London
& Groton; Who after a gallant defence, was with a part of
the brave Garrifon, inhumanly Maffacred; by britifh troops
in Fort Grifwold, Sep 6 1781 Ætatis suæ 43
By a judicious & Faithful difcharge of the various duties
of his Station, He rendered moft efential Service to his
Country; and ftood confeffed, the unfhaken Patriot;
and intrepid Hero. He lived, the Pattern of Magna
nimity; Courtefy, and Humanity. He fell the Victim
of ungenerous Rage and Cruelty.

A few yards east of the monument of Colonel Ledyard
are the following inscriptions:

Here Lies yᵉ Body of
Mʳ Daniel Chefter fon
of Mʳ Thomas Chefter
who was Killed in fort
Grifwold after he Surrendered
fepᵗ 6ᵗʰ 1781 in yᵉ 27 year of
his Age

My blood was Spilt upon yᵉ
earth, By Relentless In-
human foes I fall a Sa-
crifice to Death.

Here Lies ye Body of
Mr Eldredge Chefter fon of Mr Thomas
Chefter who was wound-
ed in fort Griswold fep^t
6th 1781 and died of his wounds dec 31st in
ye 24th year of his Age.

Relentlefs was my foe, Deaths weapons through
me went, Fell by ye Fatal blow, Lingered
till life was Spent.

In Memory of
Mr Andrew Billings
Son of Capt Stephen
& Mrs Bridget Billings
Who was Inhumanly
Maffacred by Britifh troops
in Fort Grifwold
Sepr 6th *AD* 1781
In the 22^d year
of his age.

In Memory of Lieu^t
Ebenezer Avery who
fell Glorioufly in Defence
of fort Grifwould and
American Freedom
fep^t 6th 1781 in ye 49th
year of his Age

Exhibiting a noble Specimen
of Military Valour
and Patriotic Virtue.

Sacred
to the memory of
Capt John Williams
who fell glorioufly
fighting for the
liberty of his country
in Fort Grifwold
Sep 6 1781 in the
43rd year of his age.

* * *

Ye patriot friends that weep my fate
As if untimely flain,
Faith binds my foul to Jefus's breaft
And turns my lofs to gain.

14

In Memory of
Cap' YOUNGS LEDYARD
who was mortally wounded
making heroic exertions
for the defence of
Fort Grifwold Sep' 6th
of which he died
the 7th *AD:* 1781
in the 31st year of his Age.

In the Starr Burial-ground, on the North Road, in Groton:

In Memory of
M' ELNATHAN PERKINS
who was flain at Fort
Grifwould Sep 6th 1781
in the 64 year
of his Age

Ye Britifh Power that boafts aloud
of your Great Lenity
Behold my fate when at your feet
I and three Sons muft Die.

In Memory of M[r]
Afia   Perkins   who
was flain in fort Grifwould
Sept[t] 6th 1781 in y[e] 33rd
year of his Age

Ye Britifh tyrants
that have Power '
And butchers wet
With Human Gore
Judgement muft come
And you will be
Rewarded for your
Cruelty.

In Memory of M[r]
Luke Perkins who
was flain at fort
Grifwould fep[t] 6th
1781 in y[e] 29th year
of his Age

Ye fons of Liberty
be not Difmay[d]
That I have fell
a Sacrifice to Death
But oh to think how
will their debt be paid
Who murther[d] me
when they are call[d]
from Earth.

In Memory of M[r]
Thomas Minard he
fell a victom [to] Death
the 6th of ſept 1781
in y[e] 30 year of
his Age.

My blood was ſpilt upon
the Earth, reſigned my
breath, By relentleſs
inhuman foes I fell,
a Sacrifice to Death.

In Memory of M[r] Chriſtopher Woodbridge he was
Kil'*d* in fort Griſwould ſep[t] 6
1781 in y[e] 27th
year of his Age.

In Memory of M[r]
Wait Leſter ſon of
M[r] Thomas Leſter
& Mary his wife
he fell in the
Battle at Fort
Griſwould ſep[t]
6th 1781 in y[e]
22[d] year of his Age.

In Memory of

MR HENERY WOODBRIDGE

who was flain in Fort

Grifwould Sep^t 6th 1781

in the 33^d year

of his Age.

Will not a day of reckoning come
does not my blood for vengeance cry
how will thofe wretches bear their doo^m
who haft me flain moft Murderoufly.

In Memory of M^r

Simeon Perkins

who was Slain in

fort Grifwould

fep 6th 1781 in

ye 22^d year

of his Age.

In Memory of M[r]
Elifha Perkins who
fell a Sacrifice for his
Countrys Caufe in that
horrible maffacre at fort
Grifwould fep[t] 6th
1781 in y[e] 38 year
of his Age.

Kingdoms and States
Degenerates
Keep grace forever nigh
My Blood hath ftained the
britifh fame
for their humanity.

In Memory of
M[R] NICHOLAS STARR
who was flain in Fort
Grifwould Sep[tr] 6 1781
in his 40th year

O thou Inveterate Foe
what is it thou haft done
thou ftruck the fatal blow
no mercy could be fhown

In Memory of

THOMAS STARR JU[R]

who was flain in

Fort Grifwold Sep 6th 1781

in the 19th year

of his age.

About one mile north of the Starr Cemetery, on the same road, in a small inclosure, known as the Wood Burial-Ground, is a stone bearing the following inscription:

In Memory of Cap[t] Samuel Allyn

he Departed this Life fep[t] 6 1781

in fort Grifwould by traitor Ar

nolds murdering corps in the

47 year of his Age.

By Gods decree my bounds

Ware fixt, the time y[e] place,

tho much confuf[d];

The Caufe was Good; y[e]

Means ware vile,

Snatche[d] me from Charms

of Golden Life.

The following is in the "Old Cemetery" near Gale's Ferry:

In Memory of
MR RUFUS HURLBUT
Who fell in the bloody
Committed by Benedict Arnolds troops
Massacre,at Fort Grifwould
Sept^{ber} the 6th 1781 in the 40th
year of his Age.

Reader confider how I fell
For Liberty I blead
Oh then repent ye Sons of hell
For the innocent blood you fhead

In the old Ground at Allyn's Point in Ledyard:

In Memory of Belton
Allyn¹ fon to Deaⁿ Jofeph
Allyn who fell in fort
Grifwould by traitor Ar
nolds corps fep^r 6 1781
in ye 17th year of his Age.

By Cruel rage of Britifh
man this body^{es} brought
to duft again But we
through faith do hope
this duft will rife
in triumph with ye Juft.

---

[1] On the morning of the battle this young man, in company with his Cousin Benadam, started for the fort in answer to the signal guns, as he had often before done. On their way they called upon a sister of Benadam, who was teaching school near Gale's Ferry. To her anxious inquiry of where they were going so early with their guns, Benadam

In Memory of M[r]
Benadam Allyn who died
fep[t] 6th 1781 In fort grifwould
by traitor arnalds murdering
Corps in y[e] 20th year of his Age.

To future ages this fhall
Tell This brave youth
in fort grifwould fell
For amaricas Liberty
He fought & Blead
Alas he die[d]

In Memory of Cap[t] Si
meon Allyn who Died
fep[r] 6 1781 in fort
Grifwould with his Lieu[t]
Enf[n] & 13 foldiers by trai
tor arnolds murdering Corps
in y[e] 37th year of his Age.

By Gods decree my bounds
ware fixt the time y[e]
place though much Confuf[d]
the Caufe was good y[e]
means was vile. Snatch[d]
me from Charms of
Golden Life.

---

replied, "Down to the training to see the fun." "You will never come
back alive," said she, and burst into tears.

Belton was killed on the ramparts soon after entering the works, and
before the storm. On learning of his departure, his father armed himself, and mounting his horse, followed as rapidly as possible, to share his
danger; but on his arrival found the fort invested, and he was compelled,
through the long hours of dreadful suspense, to await within hearing, the
result of the conflict, to find at last his only son a corpse.

15

In the Turner Ground in Ledyard:

In Memory of M[r]
Mofes Jones who was
flain in fo͵t Grifwould
fep' 6th 1781 in y° 25th
year of his Age

Will not a day of Rec
oning come, Does not
my blood for vengeance
Cry?   How will thofe
Wretches hear their
Doom who hath me
Slain Moft Murderoufly

In Memory of M[r] Jofeph
Moxley who Died fep[tr]
6th 1781, in fort Griswould
by traitor arnolds
murdering Corps in y°
46th year of his Age.

By Gods decree my
bounds ware fixt, the
time the place, the means
though vile, & whilft I blead,
the views of blifs, Faith
triumphed over Monfter Death.

Near Morgan's Pond, [or Sandy Hollow,] Ledyard:

In Memory of Mr Simeon
Morgan who died fep^r 6th
1781 in fort Grifwould by trai
tor arnolds murdering Corps
in ye 27^h year of his Age.

This Blooming youth in
fweets of life, his God
doth Call while Cannon
roar, a winged dart
doth feafe his breath,
& takes him from
this Golden fhore.

In Memory of Enfⁿ
John Lefter who died
fep^r 6th 1781 in fort
Grifwould by traitor
Arnolds murdering Corps
in ye 42^d year of his Age.

By Gods decree my bounds
ware fixt, the time y^e
place though much Confuf^d,
the Caufe was good y^e
means was vile, Snatch^d
me from Charms of
Golden Life

In Memory of M[r]
Andrew Baker who Died
ſep[r] 6th 1781 in fourt Griſ
would by Traitor Arnolds
Murdering Corps in the
26th year of his Age.

This gallant youth while
Cannons roar, Decree[d] by
God to live no more
a ſudden dart by mur
dering hands, Death Ceaſed
his life at Gods Command.

In Memory of
Lieut Joſeph Lewis who
died ſept[r] 6th 1781 In fourt
Griſwould by traitor Arnolds
murdering Corps in y[e] 41st
year of his Age.

This gallant man when God
Doth call doth give his life
in freedoms cauſe; a ſudden
dart doth wing away that
precious life that dwells
in Clay.

In the "Old Palmer Ground," near the head of Palmer's Cove, at Noank, is the following:

In Memory of M^r
David Palmer who
was ſlain in Fort
Griſwould ſep 6th
1781 in ye 38
year of his Age.

In the "Old Ground" at Pequonoc:

Sacred to the
Memory of M^r
Thomas Avery
ſon to Park Avery
Jn^r who made
his exit in fort
Griſwould ſep^t
6th 1781 Aged
17 years.

Life how ſhort Eternity
how long.

In Memory of Enſign
Daniel Avery who
nobly nobly Sa
crificed his Life
in Defence of fort
Griſwould & the
Liberties of America
ſep^t 6 1781 in y^e
41st year of his Age.

In Memory of M^r
Solomon Avery
who was ſlain in
fort Griſwould by
the britiſh troops
ſep^t 6th 1781 in
ye 33^d year of
his Age.

In Memory of M^r
Patric Ward who
fell a victim to
Britiſh cruelty in fort
Griſwould ſep^t 6th
1781 in ye 25th
year of his Age

In Memory of

Mr Elifha Avery

who was flain in fort Grifwould

fep^t 6 1781 in

ye 26th year of

his Age.

It is appointed

for man once

to die.

In Memory of

Mr Jafper Avery

who was flain in fort

Grifwould in defence

of his Countrys

freedom fep^t 6th

1781 in ye 38th year

of his Age.

This life uncer

tain but Death

comes to all

In Memory of
Capt Elijah Avery
who having filled up
Private and ſocial life with endearing Expreſſions
of Tenderneſs & affection
Diſplayed a moſt brave & heroic ſpirit
In defence of Fort Griſwold
and American Liberty
& fell a ſacrifice to britiſh Barbarity
Sep^{tr} 6th 1781 in the 48th
year of his Age

In Memory of
David Avery Esq^R
who having performed the endearing
Office of Friendſhip and Religion
in Social Connections;
and uſefully and honorably
ſerved the Public in various Characters;
Nobly riſk'd his life in defence of
Fort Griſwold & American Freedom;
and fell a victim to britiſh Inhumanity
Septr 6th, 1781, in the 54th
Year of his age.

In the Old Ground at Burnett's Corners, in Groton:

In
Memory of
JOHN P BABCOCK
who together with a small
party of Americans in
Fort Griswold withstood
an Assault made by a
Detachment of
British Troops
until being overcome
by superior numbers
he was Massacred
Sep^t 6th 1781
Æ 30 years.

In memory of Capt
Hubbard Burrows
who was killed
in Fort Grifwold
Sept 6th 1781
in the 42^d year
of his age.

16

In the White Hall Ground on Mystic River, in the town of Stonington:

In Memory of M^r
Thomas Williams
who was kill^d in
fourt Grifwould
fep^r 6th
AD 1781
in ye 60th year
of his age.

The following inscription is in the private ground of Seth Williams, Esq., on the "Norwich and Mystic road," in the town of Ledyard:

In Memory of
Lieut Henry Williams
fon of Capt Henry Williams
& Mary his Wife
who fell at Fort
Grifwold Sep 6th 1781
in the 32^d year of
his age.

In the first Ground in New London are those given
below.

In Memory of
Mr John Holt Junr
who was flain in Fort
Grifwold fep 6th 1781
in the 35 year of his age.

In Memory of Capt
Adam Shapley of Fort
Trumbull who brauely
gave his Life for his
Country. A fatal Wound
at Fort Grifwold Sep 6th
1781 caufed his Death
Feb^r 14 1782 Aged
45 years

Shapley thy deed reverse
the Common doom
and makes thy name
immortal in a tomb

In Memory
of Mr John Clark who departed
this life Sept 6th 1781
aged 34.

In Memory of
Lieut Richard Chapman
who was Killed at
Fort Grifwold Sep^{tr} 6th
1781 in the 45 year
of his age

How ſuddenly deaths arrows fly
They ſtrike us & they paſs not by
But hurl us to the grave.

In Memory of
Jonathan Fox[1] who
loſt his Life in de
fence of his Country
ſep^{t} 6th 1781 by
a Wound received
in his breaſt when
Courageouſly faceing
his Unnatural
Enemies & in y^{e}
30th year of his Age.

---

[1] He was doubtless killed on the west side of the river, as his name does not appear among those of the killed in Fort Griswold.

In Cedar Grove Cemetery, New London. This stone was removed from the Old Ground a few years since:

In Memory of
Capt PETER RICHARDS
who was willing to Hazzard
every danger in defence
of American Independence
was a Volunteer in
Fort Grifwold at Groton
the 6th of fept 1781
and there Slain in the
28 year of his Age.

In the Old Stanton Burial-Ground, in Stonington, are buried in one grave, two brothers; their monument bears the following inscription:

Lieut Enoch Stanton died in ye 36th year of his Age.	Serg^t Daniel Stanton died in ye 26th year of his Age.

Here intered are the bodies of two brothers
Sons of Capt Phineas Stanton and
Elizabeth his wife, who fell with many
of their friends Sep^t 6th 1781, while man
fully fighting for the liberty of their country
and in defence of Fort Grifwould.
The affailants were troops commanded
by that moft defpicable parricide,
Benedict Arnold.

In the Burial-Ground near Comstock's Wharf, in the town of Montville, is a fine granite monument, bearing the following:

Erected By
Robert Comstock Esq
to the Memory of
his Grandfather
JAMES COMSTOCK
who bravely fell
in Fort Griswold
in the Service of his Country
Sept 6 1783 [1]
Aged 75.
A signal example of valor
Patriotism and heroic virtue.

In the Old Ground on Saybrook Point:

Daniel' Son of
Cap' Charles &
M'' Temparence
Williams
who fell in the Action
in Fort Grifwould
on Groton hill on the
6th of Sep'' 1781
in the 15th year
of his Age.

[1] This boy was in Fort Griswold as a substitute for a man by the name of Kirtland, who had been drafted from the Saybrook Militia, but whose wife being sick he was excused, and Williams accepted in his stead. The price of substitution was a hogshead of cider, paid to his father by Kirtland.

He arrived at the fort only the day preceding the battle, and was killed by a rifle-shot while passing powder from the magazine to the artillerists before the assault. He was the youngest of the garrison of whom there remains a record.

His name does not appear upon the memorial tablet in the monument; why is not understood. The only reason probable is, either his late arrival followed so soon by the battle, or being a substitute his true name was not enrolled.

APPENDIX.

SEE CORRESPONDING NUMBERS IN THE LIST OF KILLED, PAGES
85, 86.

1. CAPTAIN AMOS STANTON.—Resided in the north parish of Groton, since town of Ledyard. He was an officer in the regular army, and at the time of his death at home on furlough.

Extensive inquiry and research failed to discover the place of his burial, which is supposed, however, to have been in the old and now discontinued burial-ground on the hill-side, near the residence of Charles Stanton, Esq., in Ledyard.

2. CAPTAIN NATHAN MOORE.—Lived on Groton Bank, near the ferry. There is little doubt but that his remains were interred in the Ledyard Cemetery.

3. SERGEANT JOHN STEDMAN.—Nothing is known of him, save that he died in the fort. His friends suppose him to have been buried in the old ground east of and near Gale's Ferry.

4. SERGEANT EZEKIEL BAILEY.—Probably buried in the Starr Ground.

5. SERGEANT CHRISTOPHER AVERY.—His descendants suppose him to have been interred at Poquonoc with his family.

6. CORPORAL EDWARD MILLS.—In the old ground on "Whitman Meeting-House Hill."

7. CORPORAL LUKE PERKINS, JR., son of Elnathan Perkins, buried in the Starr Ground, and whose epitaph is given in this work. He was, without doubt, buried near his father, and his grave designated by a monument, but which has now disappeared.

8. CORPORAL NATHAN SHOLES.—Nothing definite can be learned of him. He is supposed, however, by old inhabitants, to have been buried in the "Sandy Hollow" Ground, in Ledyard, near which his family resided.

9. SYLVESTER WALWORTH, buried in Ledyard Cemetery. His grave is known to have been left unprovided with memorial stones.

10, 11. PHILLIP COVIL and JEDEDIAH CHESTER.—Of these men nothing can be learned.

12. DAVID SEABURY, a relative of Bishop Seabury. The family lived in Ledyard, near Poquetanock, where his unmarked grave is supposed to be.

13. JOHN BROWN.—Nothing known.

14. NATHAN ADAMS.—Lived in the section of Groton known as "Gungewamps," where, in a thickly wooded valley, is a rough, uncut slab of granite, upon which are rudely engraved the initials N. A. Tradition says this stone was prepared by Adams previous to his death, and after that event, in accordance with his desire, it was placed, by his friends, at his grave.

15. SAMUEL HILL.—Nothing known of him; probably a transient inhabitant of Groton.

16. JONAS LESTER.—Probably buried near his cousin, Ensign John Lester, in the "Sandy Hollow" Ground. Nothing definite known.

17. JOHN BILLINGS.—Is thought to have belonged to North Stonington. Nothing can be ascertained regarding the place of his sepulture.

18, 19, 20. JOSEPH WEDGER, SAMUEL BILLINGS, and ELIDAY JONES, unknown.

21. THOMAS LAMB.—In the ancient ground on "Whitman Meeting-House Hill," Groton.

17

22. FREDERICK CHESTER.—Not certainly known, but very probably was buried with his relatives in the Starr Ground.

23, 24. DANIEL DAVIS and DANIEL B. LESTER, unknown. So far as can be ascertained, Lester was not connected with the families to which John, Jonas, and Wait belonged.

25. SOLOMON TIFT.—His name does not appear upon the tablet in the monument, but is found in the list of killed published in the Connecticut Gazette of September 21st, 1781, which, so far as complete, is undoubtedly correct. There are those of the same name and probably of the same family now residing in Groton, but the place of his interment can not be ascertained.

If to this name we add those of Jedediah [or Jeremiah in the Gazette] Chester and Daniel Williams, also not upon the tablet, we reconcile the apparent inconsistency between Arnold's official report, which gives the number found dead in the fort as eighty-five, and the monumental list of the same number, but which is known, however, to include the names of three who died subsequent to the enemy's departure, viz: Adam Shapley, Eldredge Chester, and Youngs Ledyard; thus making a total of eighty-eight slain, instead of eighty-five, as heretofore supposed.

26. BENONI KENSON.—Credited to New London. No representative of the family has resided in the neighborhood for many years. He is said to have been a sailor attached to one of the privateer vessels lying in the harbor at the time, and volunteered for the defense of the fort. If so, he was doubtless interred in the Old Ground at New London.

27, 28. JONATHAN BUTLER and WILLIAM BOLTON, known to have been buried in the last-named ground.

29. WILLIAM COMSTOCK, a member of Captain Shapley's company, was probably buried in the Comstock Ground, in Montville.

30, 31. ELIAS COIT and BARNEY KINNEY, in the first ground at New London.

32. CAPTAIN ELIAS H. HALSEY was captain of a privateer brig lying in the harbor. He was probably from Bridgehampton, Long Island, where many of the name still reside.

33, 34. JOHN WHITTLESEY, (aged 23,) and his half brother, STEPHEN WHITTLESEY, (16,) although originally credited to New London, are known to have belonged to that part of Saybrook now constituting the town of Westbrook. They were drafted from the militia of that town for the defense of New London Harbor, and were members of Captain Shapley's company of artillery, stationed in Fort Trumbull. Their burialplace is not definitely known, but it is highly probable that it is near that of an elder brother, (Joseph,) whose monument is found in the cemetery at Westbrook Village.

35. SAMBO LATHAM, unknown.

36. JORDAN FREEMAN.—He was the body servant of Colonel Ledyard, and buried in the Ledyard Cemetery.

FINIS.